I0729259

HERE

EARTHBOUND FANTASIES AND FUTURES

NICKY PENTTILA

HERE

CONTENTS

INTRODUCTION
LOOKING CLOSE TO HOME

There's a particular quality of attention that children have before we teach them not to use it. They notice that certain shadows fall wrong. They see patterns adults have learned to ignore. They ask why the air tastes different in some rooms, why some silence feels heavier than others.

Most of us lose this way of seeing. We're taught that the world operates according to known rules, that mysteries have explanations, that strange experiences are just our minds playing tricks. We learn to look past inconsistencies, to rationalize the uncanny, to file away observations that don't quite fit.

The stories in this collection are for those who never quite stopped noticing.

They take place in the United States we know—or think we know. Small towns perched on harsh coastlines. Cities rebuilt from industrial collapse. Universities with libraries that sprawl deeper than their blueprints suggest. The settings are mundane, even bureaucratic: daycare centers, art galleries, research stations. Places where people go about their daily work, maintaining the systems that keep society functioning.

But something is always slightly off. Not wrong enough to raise alarms, just wrong enough to raise questions. The kind of questions that, once asked, change how you see everything else.

These aren't tales of chosen ones or grand destinies. Just folks doing their jobs, caring for their families, trying to get by. They become involved with the fantastic not through prophecy but through proximity—because they happened to be present when the ordinary revealed its other face. What they discover doesn't make them special. It makes them responsible.

This is fantasy grounded in the complexity of real life, where solutions create new problems, where even small revelations can restructure a life, where the line between blessing and burden depends entirely on your perspective. The magic here doesn't offer escape from human concerns—it amplifies them, complicates them, makes them impossible to ignore.

For the world is far stranger than we acknowledge, that our careful boundaries between possible and impossible are more fragile than we pretend, that paying attention—really paying attention—is itself a form of magic.

Welcome to Earth, that familiar strange place. Take a look. You might be surprised by what's been here all along.

THE WITNESS

MOM LIKED to sit on the porch for hours. It was like watching television, she'd said to Katie, only slow enough that she could follow it.

Worked for Katie. Their narrow city suburb street had almost no traffic, and Mom didn't seem bothered by the leaf blowers in fall and the lawn mowers in spring and summer. She even sat out there, all bundled up, on the milder winter days.

Mom loved to keep up with the quiet lives of her Hyattsville, Maryland, neighbors, most of whom rolled out of the neighborhood in their black or gray SUVs before eight and didn't return until five or six. In the meantime, there were always the dog walkers, the stroller set, and the solitary people hustling down the shallow hill to the bus stop on the corner or walking more slowly up the incline with their groceries or just the weight of their cares.

Katie didn't have to worry about Mom going off the porch. Aretha Godwin was afraid of the six steep brick steps to their lawn now; she preferred to go down the wooden stairs to the basement and out the garage door. Hard to believe she had been a dancer and teacher for forty years, unafraid of any leap. But that was a long time ago.

They left the window in the living room that looked out to the porch open, so Mom could call if she needed anything. Katie's office window also faced the front of the house, so she cracked that one open, too, just in case. Not much she could do if she heard something wrong while she was on a conference call, but it helped her worry less.

Katie stepped out onto their porch carrying an insulated tumbler with a built-in straw of watery coffee for Mom and her own cellphone for the office. Ten minutes before her next conference call—project managing from home was a trip, but she was lucky to have the job so she couldn't complain.

It was perfect on the porch. The sun had risen past the point where it blazed straight into the windows, and now the big oak tree in the apron of their yard and the dogwood to the left offered plenty of dappled shade. The dogwood still had its little white spring flowers, their soft, apple-mango scent coloring the air.

Mom sat in her faded pine Adirondack chair, cozied into the cushions Katie had bought new at Christmas. They should repaint it again; the blue had worn into gray along the wide armrests and tall back of the chair. Katie's matching chair didn't really match—no cushions and gray all over. She couldn't afford to sit out here long.

Mom's short gray curls lay flat this morning. She liked it short, she said, so the wind could fluff it if it wanted to. She had on her black ballet flats, her favorite brown corduroy swing skirt and a creamy blue sweater set. Katie had had to search for elbow patches that came close to that color. Luckily, Mom didn't notice stuff like that anymore.

Until she did.

Spring was the best. Comfortable if you were wearing a sweater, no bugs—and no humidity. They sat only a mile from the border with Washington, DC, which was not built on a swamp but on a riverbank with a few tidal flats. But the humidity didn't make fine distinctions like that, and once it kicked on in May it was a sauna until September.

But they were used to it now. Mom and Dad had moved in when she got the professor job at University of Maryland, back when a teacher and a union plumber could afford a house here. When Katie grew up here, the neighborhood was full of kids, running in and out of each other's postage-stamp lawns, finding shade on the west side of the street in the mornings, and the east side in the afternoons. Then everyone grew up and left, and the block grew quiet and gray. But a new set of toddlers had moved in two years ago, and another couple had had a baby, so now the shrieking and laughter and chalk on the narrow sidewalks were back.

Katie waved the coffee tumbler in front of Mom until she focused on it, and then set it on the right armrest of Mom's chair. Mom put her hand around the tumbler and smiled at it. Not the sad smile, but the happy one.

Katie dropped into her own chair, in the center of the tiny porch, directly behind the big bush next to the stairs. Overgrown again, it hid her from direct view, which she liked. Mom liked her chair to be in the far corner, looking over the much-smaller bush, so she could see everything.

They looked out and across (or diagonally, in Katie's case), to the matching sets of boxy 1950s red-brick houses. Same rabbit-warren first floors, same two dormer windows on the second floors, but slightly different trim on each. Some had wooden railings on cement porches, others, like them, black metal railings and roof supports over brick porches. Most folks had remodeled the second floor into living space, rather than attic, and many of the side windows held air conditioners because nobody's "whole-house" AC could keep up.

Katie could distinguish at least three kinds of bird calls. The cheep-cheep birds were long-termers, along with the deep-throated crows and the whistles and chatter of the orioles. But that one that sounded like a car alarm, that one was migratory and it could migrate itself out of here right now.

"I saw something," Mom said. "At Elaine Halliday's."

Katie closed her eyes to keep from rolling them. Mom couldn't remember what she'd had for dinner last night but she would not let go of the idea that Professor Halliday's house was haunted.

Professor Halliday (history, Early Middle Ages, Eurasia) kept her green grass lawn perfect. Her porch had a triangle roof, which with the two dormer windows, one on each side of the porch, made her little square brick house look like a pig, at least to five-year-old Katie. Her wooden porch, with its vertical slat railing was painted white, like the frames of her six-pane sashed windows. She had no garage attached, and just two narrow cement lines with grass in between were her driveway. There was nothing special about her house.

Except the cat, an indoor-outdoor sleek gray-black monster. When she wanted to be let in, Minnie the cat would leap up to the first-floor window in front, and sit on the narrow brick ledge until Professor Halliday noticed it.

Minnie wasn't there now, in the middle of her busy morning, obviously. No one was on the porch, with its two white Adirondack chairs with the matching square table between. Despite the nice chairs, Professor Halliday wasn't really a porch person.

"It was the colors, again," Mom said. She took a sip of her coffee through the metal straw with the rubber tip. "They seemed to wash out of Minnie's window like a rainbow spraying from a hose."

Katie leaned past the bush to look at the house. Was there some trick of the light that could prism the sun into a rainbow? She didn't see it.

"Sounds pretty."

"No!" Mom sat straighter. Her hands started to flutter.

Shit.

"Okay," Katie said soothingly. "Tell me more?"

The hands drifted back down to Mom's lap. "Sprayed out. And then the boy ran out, like his hair was on fire."

The boy was a thirty-something skinny white man, dark floppy hair, who always looked like he was about to explode. When Mom had first seen him, he'd upset her just by scowling at Minnie. Katie had had to knock on Professor Halliday's door and inquire about the young man just to set Mom's mind at ease again. The professor (neat, gray, rose-scented) was friendly enough, but talking with her you always got the idea that she'd be much happier if she never had to talk to you again.

"Eli? The professor's post-doc?" Katie asked.

"And the colors followed him all the way to the street, where his little gray car was." Mom's eyes were glazed with memory. Her hands went busy again, curving like a rounded roof. "His car turned blue! And his hair went green."

Neither his hair nor his car were to be seen on the street now. "Poor guy," Katie said.

Her mother waved her concern away. "It was already fading by the time he got the car started. But look!" She pointed to the street. "He left skid marks, he left so fast."

Katie had to stand to see over the bush at the street in front of them. Yes, there were fresh tire marks near the curb in front of Professor Halliday's house.

"And you know," Mom continued, "Elaine wasn't home."

That did seem odd. But Katie's phone alarm went off, time for the meeting.

After a busy day corralling people in the throes of convention prep, and a frustrating foray into the kitchen for dinner (she finally ordered out, again), Katie had forgotten the whole thing.

Almost.

THE NEXT MORNING—SATURDAY!—KATIE stood in the living room near the outside door, trying to decide what and how much she could take out of this room without her Mom noticing. It was crazy that they had five bookcases in here, dominating the room, overflowing with books, folded maps, little ceramic dancers, and what-all. Four of them took up one whole wall, the two tall brown oak ones banged together in the middle, with two white pressed-wood ones tucked under the windows on each side.

The other tall oak bookcase stood against the wall into the

rest of the house, next to one of the two black-leather push-back reclining chairs. This chair, with its wide wood armrests that could hold a coffee cup on a woven coaster, was Mom's. It looked straight out past the rust-colored futon couch under the front window and onto the porch and the rest of the neighborhood. The other recliner, kitty-corner from Mom's, was Katie's, and it looked onto the four bookshelves, and their chaos.

Not chaos for long. Katie loaded one of her three empty medium-sized packing boxes onto the matching dark-oak coffee table and set to work. Last weekend, she'd cleared off the coffee table, and it was still clear, so that was good. Those yellowing paperbacks on the top shelf all had print so small neither of them could read it anymore. As Katie swept the first handful off the shelf and into the box, holding her breath against the dust, she heard Mom greet someone outside. A short "halloo," so probably a sidewalk stroller.

Then she heard the sharp knock on the door.

She wiped her hands on the sides of her jeans and skirted the coffee table to get to the door. She glanced out the window. Mom was calm, giving whoever was behind the door a shy smile. Her hair was dancing in the wind. Wasn't this supposed to be a no-wind, bad-for-sailing day?

Two people who reminded Katie of birds stood on the porch. Bright eyes, twitchy faces. She expected them to chirp, but the taller one spoke in a normal human voice.

"Katie Harris," they said.

"It's Godwin, again," Katie said with an apologetic smile. So yeah, getting divorced meant she had to sleep in her childhood room again, but at least now she had a bathroom to herself. And Mom could have cheaper in-home care.

"Katie Godwin," the tall person said. Dressed head to to in black crepey-looking fabric, like a washed-out undertaker, with stiff laced leather shoes and a voice to match. "We have need of your parlor."

Katie looked over her shoulder, squinted. Still a boring, overstuffed living room. "Parlor?"

"Ah…" They looked at the shorter one, the one that carried all the color. Red swoopy hair, bright yellow raincoat over a pink ruffled t-shirt and green camo overalls, shiny black Doc Martens.

"Living room," that one said.

"I don't understand," Katie said. "Do we know you?" Had Mom forgotten to tell her that friends were coming to visit? But Katie knew all of Mom's friends, who were all pretty much Mom's age. These two looked younger. And weirder.

The red-headed one grinned. "No need, we're merely asking you to stand as host on account of neutral geography and your mother's status as a witness."

"Witness?" Katie glanced at her Mom, who was still smiling dreamily at their guests.

"May we come in?" the colorful one asked, already nudging past her into the living room. The taller one followed, glancing at the shelves of books as if cataloguing evidence.

Mom, still seated on the porch, craned her neck to watch, then nodded decisively. She pushed herself up and tottered into the living room, patting Katie on the arm as she passed in a swirl of baby powder and suntan lotion. Same brown skirt, but the butter yellow sweater set today. Mom made her way to the window instead of to her usual chair—the strangers stood between her and the chair—and sat at the far right edge of the futon sofa. Her deep pumpkin corduroy skirt matched the futon cover perfectly. She'd made them both, way back.

"I—do we need a lawyer?" Katie asked, suddenly aware she was in her rattiest red Maryland sweatshirt and her hair was a mess.

The living room rippled, as if she'd blinked and missed a jump cut. The air fizzed, and suddenly the space rearranged itself. Her big leather chair scooted itself over to sit shoulder-to-shoulder with Mom's against the back wall. The round metal stool with the cracked blue leather seat from the kitchen appeared, set against what used to be the bank of bookshelves, now bare of anything but the off-white paint on the walls.

All of their full-to-bursting bookcases had vanished. As had the three moving boxes. And the coffee table.

"Books are distracting," said the tall stranger. "They can return once order is restored."

Katie took a step back, banging into the still-open front door. The birds outside cheeped and cawed. The little girls next door screeched and laughed. And Professor Halladay was at the door, with Arda the neighborhood's best cleaning lady, in tow.

"Katherine," the professor said, nodding her perfectly coiffed head at Katie before stepping over the threshold. She led Arda, usually a ruddy white lady with energy to spare but today a little wide-eyed and pale, over to the futon. The professor looked dressed for an academic seminar, black slacks, emerald silk blouse, practical flats. Roses. Arda, in black running shorts and a Metallic Anchor t-shirt, looked like she'd been out for a jog and was seriously thinking of taking up sprinting, right this second.

Mom smiled at them both. "Nice to meet you," she said to Arda, who sat next to her.

Arda's shoulders eased; her return smile was genuine and sweet. Mom never remembered Arda, but was always happy to see her, once every two weeks, to clean the house.

"Oh, isn't this clever!" Mom trilled, surveying the transformed room. "Look, Katie—we haven't had so much space since your fifth birthday!" A cloud crossed her face. "But Bruce —he won't like it."

That answer, Katie knew. "Dad won't mind, Mom. He suggested it." He wouldn't complain about the white lie: Bruce Godwin had been gone for eight and a half years.

She pushed the door shut. She'd had enough.

Sometime in the time between entering the room and the time they settled themselves on the side-by-side recliners, the strangers had donned robes like the kind judges wore. If judges wore cream-silken robes with runes or something in green along the collars and hems.

"Are we ready?" said the taller one.

Before anyone could answer, a sharp, static pop crackled in the air, and Eli materialized atop the padded stool by the naked wall. Eyes rimmed red, hands clenched together in his lap, scowl scary and also, somehow, scared.

Katie could only gape, knees wobbling. Her mind clutched for logic and found only fuzz. She stepped back, and her heel hit the short step to the landing that led to the stairs upstairs. She sank onto the step.

Outside, Minnie the cat pressed her broad face against the front window screen, green eyes wide, as if she'd been summoned for this, too.

The tall judge gave a dramatic, ceremonial sigh, set their

stiff leather-shod feet flat on the floor, and straightened their robe.

"For the record. You are assembled as follows: Elaine Halliday, aggrieved party; Arda Lenz and Aretha Godwin, potential witnesses. Elijah Bainer, respondent. Katherine Godwin, householder and host. We are Cassandra Banks, chief justice. Assisted by Justices Melinda Moss," she gestured at the small bright person next to her. "And Minnetonka Smith," she nodded toward the cat on the window ledge. "Tribunal in session."

Katie gasped. She stared at Minnie, sitting regally on the brick windowsill. Then again, that cat always did seem too clever by half.

Justice Moss could not place her feet on the floor and still stay in the seat. Instead, her flaming hair bouncing, she pushed the recliner back to nearly horizontal, and then crossed her legs, tucking her boots into the folds of the robe.

Katie winced. Somebody was going to have real trouble geting those scuff marks out of silk.

"Quite finished?" Justice Banks asked Justice Moss. She nodded cheerily, not fazed by the taller justice's tone.

"We are gathered because the order of magic and of memory in this neighborhood has been disturbed," Justice Banks intoned. "There is evidence—a signature of reality shifted. It appears that an object of exceptional value was used when it should not have been. The fabric of the everyday has frayed. The tribunal requires testimony. We must, in the due course of justice, restore what was broken, reveal what was hidden, and secure the balance between the commonplace and the extraordinary."

She fixed each person—Katie, Elaine, Arda, Mom, Eli—

with a steady, expectant look. Katie was ready to spill everything—the time she snuck out to a drinking party. The time she stole five dollars from her Mom's purse just to buy a box of candy hearts on sale after Valentine's Day. The times she let her soon-to-be-ex-husband believe that it was his idea that they should break up.

Instead, the justice said, "We will begin with Elaine Halliday. Please tell the court what occurred as it appeared to you this past day."

Professor Halliday, perched stiffly at the far end of the futon, pressed her lips together. "I arrived home at a quarter past noon. I had been teaching all morning. When I opened my door, I was… startled. My living room was—" She hesitated, searching for the right word. "Splattered. All over the walls and ceiling, as if a child had gone wild with a box of paints. The air smelled like chalk and bitter lemon. My books had been reorganized by color, not subject, and some of the spines were written in languages I don't even recognize. The television was playing, but the screen only showed shifting, swirling colors."

Arda broke in: "It was nothing like that when I finished cleaning. Ten-thirty, like always, was fine. I dusted, washed, vacuumed, everything, like always. It was the second trip of the month, so I did the fridge, too."

The chief justice's gaze flicked to her. Arda shivered. She rubbed her hands on her bare knees for warmth. Mom put one of her warm, soft hands over Arda's closest hand, patting softly.

"Were you alone in the house?" the justice asked.

"No, Eli was there. He was working in the professor's office. I saw him when I was cleaning the hall."

All eyes turned to Eli, perched on the stool, looking even paler. He raised his hands, palms out. "I don't even know what's going on! I was just working. I didn't see anything weird. Maybe the TV was acting up, but I didn't touch it. I left before noon, like always."

"You left early," Halliday said, voice sharp. "You weren't there when I returned, and we were supposed to review your thesis abstract, Eli. It's due Monday, and you never showed up."

Eli's eyes darted between the judges and Halliday. "I—I wasn't feeling well. I thought I'd come back later. Look, I promise, nothing was out of the ordinary when I left."

THE SHORTER JUDGE LEANED FORWARD. "Elaine. Did you notice anything else unusual?"

"Minnie was home. She never comes home until dinner time." Minnie sitting on the window sill between Halladay and Arda, nodded.

"Yes," Justice Banks said. "Minnetonka reported the … occurrence." She peered sternly at the professor. "I was surprised that you, yourself, did not."

Professor Halladay reared back a little, her face shocked. Her hand went to the open throat of her blouse. "You're blaming me?"

"Carelessness can also be a crime."

Justice Moss nodded agreement. A shaft of sunlight from the side window caught the movement, making her red hair sparkle. "Objects that carry magic weight greater than eight are to be kept under lock and key. I understand this object was found on the floor beside your desk?"

Professor Halladay turned to glare at Minnie, behind her.

The chief judge waved a hand, catching all their attention. "So. We have a house in magical disarray, a witness who saw the space in perfect order at half past ten, and a respondent who claims ignorance. Is there anyone else who entered the house, Professor Halliday?"

"No."

"Do you have anything else to add to your testimony?"

"The pen was on the floor." The professor sighed. "Still humming from use." She glared at the two justices in front of her. "But it hadn't been used long. The leak was contained. It didn't even get into the yard. I don't see what all the fuss is about."

The justice tapped her toe on the floor, twice. "The facts are presented. What is required now," he said, turning to Mom, "is the perspective of one who saw what others did not. Mrs. Godwin, will you tell us what you witnessed from your porch?"

Katie's heart skipped. They couldn't possibly want to rely on Mom's testimony. Could they?

Little Justice Moss turned to Mom with a gentleness that surprised everyone. "Mrs. Godwin, do you remember what you saw from your porch yesterday morning?"

Mom blinked, her gaze clouded. She glanced at Katie for help, hands twisting in her lap. "I'm ... not sure," she murmured. "I know I saw something... but what? You say colors? Maybe colors." She trailed off, shoulders drawing inward.

Justice Moss nodded briskly, as if she'd expected this. "Such barriers can be gently lifted. With your permission, Mrs. Godwin, I can help you recall just this one day. It won't last—

memories like these are like birds, easily startled—but for a short while, I promise: you'll remember exactly as you did when it happened."

Mom looked at Katie, questioning.

If only.

Katie nodded, swallowing against the tightness in her throat.

Justice Moss scrambled off her recliner and knelt before Mom, so their eyes were level. "Look at me, Aretha. Deeply. Don't look away until you see yourself, whole and strong, as you were. As you are."

A hush settled over the room; even Minnie the cat froze, tail flicking once, green eyes unblinking.

Katie's breath caught as her mother's posture changed. The uncertain way Mom had held herself for so long faded, replaced by a new poise. No, a familiar poise. Her spine straightened, her shoulders fell in place. Her chin lifted. A prima ballerina, again. Even her voice, when it came, was stronger, truer.

Her own.

"I remember," Mom said, quietly but distinctly.

Justice Moss nodded, rising. "Tell us, please."

Mom drew a breath. "I was sitting on the porch, as I often do, watching the street and all the people. It was late morning; the light was soft, not too bright. Perfect spring day. I saw Eli come out of Elaine's house. He was moving fast, almost running. There were colors—colors I'd never seen—pouring out of the window after him. Not like a rainbow. More like… paint thrown in water, swirling and chasing. The colors followed him right out the door, down the steps, and into the street."

Katie hadn't heard Mom talk at length, and so easily, in years. On the stair, she hugged herself, promising herself to remember this Mom, always. Even on the hard days.

Justice Moss walked back to her recliner—Katie's recliner—and perched herself atop it again.

Mom closed her eyes, searching. "When he got to his car, it —changed. The color shifted, from gray to blue to green, and back to gray. Eli's hair flashed green, just for a second. Whatever the wave was, it looked like it had washed itself out." She looked at Eli. "And then he drove off so fast he left skid marks. On our street."

She looked at Katie, blinking. "I thought I was seeing things. I knew you didn't believe me."

A hush fell. Arda, next to Mom, took her hand and held it, hard. Katie, pressing a hand to her chest, found tears in her eyes, half joy, half grief.

Katie cleared her throat, looking at her hands, twisting in her lap. "She's right. She told me all this yesterday. A garden hose spewing color from the window, something like that. Just before my noon meeting."

And Katie hadn't believed her.

Justice Moss nodded with approval. She looked at the chief justice. "Testimony confirmed by a second party. The memory is true."

Justice Banks smiled, maybe gently but still kind of grim, at Mom. "Thank you, Mrs. Godwin. That is a great help."

A ripple of relief, awe, and sadness moved through the room. Katie watched her mother, luminous for who knew how much longer, and wished she could hold onto it forever.

Justice Banks now turned to Eli, her gaze sharp enough it seemed to fix him to the wall like a bug.

"Elijah Bainer, you have heard the testimony and seen the evidence. Do you wish to speak for yourself?"

Eli was hugging himself so hard Katie was afraid his polo shirt would tear. "I didn't know. I swear! I knew the pen was charmed, but I thought that was it. Who would expect a power-ten artifact to be lying around on someone's desk?"

Justice Banks glared at Professor Halladay, but Justice Moss frowned at Eli.

"So you know what it is, now," said Justice Moss, crossing her arms to match her crossed legs. She tilted her head. "Looked it up, did you?"

"I thought it could give me a boost. Just a little boost. Get me on track for my dissertation." He spread his hands. "It's due, and I'm stalled out. Blocked."

Professor Halliday's lips pressed into a thin, disappointed line. "You knew it was special. You knew the rules. You should have spoken to me."

"She's right," Eli said. "Prof Halladay said not to use it. It's not her fault. I wasn't trying to hurt anyone. I never took it out of the house. I just… I needed help."

Eli's voice broke. "I thought if I could just write one good thing, just once, maybe I could finally… belong here. I'm so tired of feeling like I'm failing." His gaze dropped. "But the pen just exploded with color, no ideas at all." He sighed. "Couldn't even do that right."

Justice Moss spoke gently but firmly. "You did not steal the object. But you used it in full knowledge it was not yours, and you ignored the warnings you sensed. The magical balance in this neighborhood was disturbed. The consequences, even if unintended, were real."

Eli clasped his hands together. He brought his hands to his

lips, as if praying. Or asking for mercy. He started to rock, forward and back. The hard lines of his face, so used to scowling, seemed to soften.

There was a rap at the door, three quick taps.

"Enter!" Justice Banks called out.

Katie had forgotten to lock the door, but she suspected it wouldn't have mattered.

In stepped a compact, no-nonsense woman in orange coveralls. She had a giant leather-looking duffel bag slung from her shoulder that was wider at the short ends than her hips. She carried the slightest smell of smoke.

Probably a witch.

They were everywhere.

"Mistress Wren," Justice Banks said. "How did you fare?"

"Two hours, scrubbing out color echoes and untangling the so-called laws of physics in that office. Do you know how hard it is to get the aftertaste of lemon and static out of silk-weave carpets?"

"You deodorized that carpet?" Arda looked impressed. "And didn't stain it? How—oh. Never mind."

Wren caught sight of Eli. "You," she said. "Need a good cleaning."

Eli, eyes wide, jaw stiff, leaned back in the stool, as if he trying to get away.

Justice Banks tapped the floor again. "Elijah Bainer, do you wish to remain in the university's wizard-track program?"

The what? Maryland had a wizard-track program? Katie rubbed her forehead, her head positively stuffed with new angles on her world.

"Yes," Eli whispered. "Please."

"Do you promise to follow the instructions of your mentor, to the letter?"

Eli glanced at Professor Halladay, paused. Of course, wizarding would be in the history department. Where else would they put it? Chemistry? Katie forced her thoughts back to the proceedings.

"Yes," he said.

"Adequate." Justice Banks stood, suddenly so tall her head nearly touched the ceiling.

Now everybody reared back.

"Your punishment, Elijah Bainer, is as follows. Any magical insight you gained from the pen will be erased. Further, you are sentenced to serve our community directly. You will assist Mistress Wren"—she nodded at the magical cleaner-upper—"in restoring balance wherever it is disturbed, for as long as the council deems necessary. She will be your supervisor, and you will do as she instructs."

Eli lifted his head, relief and shame warring on his face. "I... I understand." Shame won out, and despair. "I don't think I can do it."

Professor Halliday, after a pause, spoke quietly. "Eli. You have all the makings of a fine mage. You need to learn patience. We'll learn together."

Eli looked at her, blinking hard. "Thank you."

Wren smirked. "Starts now, kid. Let's get you cleaned up. And take a look at that car of yours."

The chief justice rapped the floor with the heel of her shoe. "So ordered. Anything more?" She looked to Justice Moss, who shook her head, and then to Minnie the cat, who flicked her tail and then hopped down from the widow sill.

"Then I declare this tribunal closed." She stood, and then

had to wait for Justice Moss to push her recliner up to the seated position and slide off it. Chief Justice Banks strode over to Katie, who scrambled to stand up from the stair step.

"We are grateful for your hospitality," Banks said. She slid out of her cloak, and then folded it so many times it was small enough to fit in her black suit coat pocket. Katie goggled at that a moment—really efficient for doing laundry—before remembering to open the door for her.

"Two more things," Justice Moss said, swinging her hips as if to get the kinks out. She folded her own cloak origami-style while Wren and Eli also cleared out, Eli not looking at anyone. Then she stomped over to Arda on the sofa.

Behind the justice, the bookcases and furniture shimmied back to their rightful places, and the parlor became, once again, just a living room—albeit one that felt, for a moment, a little bigger, and a little stranger, than before.

"Madam Arda, how are you feeling?"

Arda, who hadn't let go of Mom's hand, now dropped it, staring around at the changing room.

"A little woozy," she said. "Is this really happening?" Arda looked back at Katie's Mom. Already the light was fading from Mom's eyes. Already her face was slackening. Her posture.

"I can help you to forget, just this hour, if you want." Justice Moss knelt in front of her. "It helps."

No way Katie was letting anybody take today's memories.

"And Aretha?" Arda spoke to the justice but looked at Katie. "You can help her?"

Justice Moss pursed her lips. "That's not as easy. Might not be possible at all. Fixing you," she tapped on Arda's knee, "and giving a boost to her," she tapped on Mom's knee, "takes just the tiniest bit of energy. A price I pay."

But it could be done?

Katie flung herself across the room. "You can do it?"

The sparkle left Justice Moss's eyes. "The cost is too high, dear. Be happy she is still with you."

But she wasn't still with them. Seeing Mom in those moments of clarity made it obvious that her everyday was the cruelest shadow.

Justice Moss gazed deep into Arda's eyes. The living room stilled.

The bookcases stood where they always had, as if nothing had ever moved. Arda blinked, shook her head, and suddenly seemed only tired. She squeezed Mom's hand and excused herself, muttering something about needing to check on her next client.

Katie dropped onto the sofa, still warm from Arda. She reached for one of Mom's hands, cool silk skin. "Do it," she said.

"Be sure," Moss said, soft. "This magic is nearly a direct exchange. If you wish, we can restore a piece of your mother's mind—a sliver, or perhaps more. It doesn't have to be much. Sometimes it's just a song you won't remember, a favorite flavor, a color that fades. Or," her face grew serious, "it can mean giving up whole branches of memory. Years, even. The more you give, the more she gets back."

Katie looked at her Mom. Saw the light she loved fading. The perfect posture slumping. Always the love, but soon that horrible mask of fearful uncertainty would drape itself over her again.

She turned away from Mom to look at the flame-haired magician.

"Take it," she said. "I have plenty."

Moss looked at her hard, deep, as if trying to read her mind. Or her soul. Then the magician knelt in front of Katie and took a deep breath.

But Mom spoke first. "No," she said. Firm. Angry, even.

Katie, startled, started to pull away. But Mom squeezed her hand, hard. The scent of her hand lotion—cocoa butter like the beach—grew stronger with her grip.

Mom looked right at her, eyes sharper than they'd been in years. "Don't, baby girl."

The cheep-cheep birds were screeching in the yard. Minnie must be back. The little girls next door shrieked with laughter and burbling chatter. Inside, on the sofa, silence.

"It's nothing," Katie said, shrugging as if the idea didn't frighten her. It wasn't that much a sacrifice; nothing like what Mom had sacrificed for her over the years. She hoped. "A little forgetfulness for me, for so many more bright days for you.

"Absolutely not." Mom glared at Justice Moss. "I refuse."

"Mom…"

But Mom shook her head, fierce. "No."

Justice Moss stood and brushed imaginary dust from her camo overalls. Katie stood automatically to accompany Moss to the door. After she closed the door, Katie didn't hear the magician go down the steps. The only person she'd heard go down the steps was Arda.

She rested her forehead on the cool metal of the door. She closed her eyes a moment.

Then she pushed back, put her game face on, and looked at her mother.

Mom looked around, confused by the sudden return of clutter and books. The three empty cardboard boxes were back on the coffee table. The coffee table was back. Mom blinked up at Katie, her hands fluttering, uncertain.

"Is it time for lunch?" she asked, her voice thin and sweet. "Have you seen my butter sweater? The one with the buttons?"

Katie swallowed, blinking away the sting of tears. She knelt beside her mother, tucking a stray curl behind her ear. "You're wearing it, Mom. You look beautiful."

She rested her head on Mom's thigh, taking comfort in the soft ridges of her skirt against her cheek. The house too quiet, the world both smaller and stranger than before.

Outside, a breeze shifted the new green leaves. Katie looked past Mom to see Minnie the cat strolling across the porch, tail high, pausing to look up at the window. For a heartbeat, her fur shimmered with impossible colors—chartreuse, violet, gold—before settling back to ordinary cobalt gray.

Katie smiled, just a little.

FLOATERS

MAYA LED her chattering preschoolers on a roundabout path across the playground to get to the swings and the climbers, their little sneakers and sandals springing slightly on the green-and-black poured rubber. The flexible walking rope they all held onto followed a serpentine pattern that might have seemed random to anyone watching. But Maya knew better.

"This way, everybody!" she called, voice bright as today's sun as she guided them around a large, oil-slick blob hovering five feet above the ground. It was almost dinner-plate sized today, with that telltale zigzag tail that made her stomach clench. Those were the dangerous ones. "Like little ducklings!"

The children giggled, their faces upturned and curious as they carefully traced her path. Sixteen tiny bodies swerved in perfect formation around the invisible obstacle. To them, it was just another playground game, one of Ms. Maya's special follow-the-leader adventures.

"Look!" Eliza shrieked, pointing at the floater. "A ghost!"

Maya smiled down at the four-year-old, squeezing her shoulder gently. "That's right, honey. Very good eyes."

From the bench in the shadow of Happy Toddler Daycare of Cleveland's side wall, Ms. Diane checked her watch and sighed. Maya could see the exhaustion in the droop of her co-teacher's face, her whole body. Her new baby wasn't sleeping, so nobody in the family was. Plus this heat and humidity was getting to everyone. July needed to give them a break.

"MAYA," Diane said, closing her eyes, rubbing her temples, "can we just get them to the swings one time without this whole production?"

"Almost there," Maya replied, guiding the children around another smaller blob. This one made a sound like chalk breaking against a blackboard.

"For heaven's sake," Diane muttered, pushing herself up from the bench. "I'll meet you there."

Maya held her breath as Diane started walking directly toward the large zigzag floater. She opened her mouth to warn her, but stopped—she'd learned long ago what happened when she tried to explain what she saw. The concerned looks. The suggested therapist appointments. The whispers.

Diane strode right through the floater. Maya winced as it happened—the squiggle-jelly mass rippling as her colleague passed through. Pepper and burnt sugar wafted toward Maya. Burnt energy, more like.

The effect was immediate. Diane's shoulders slumped further, her pace slowed, and the color seemed to drain from her face. She stumbled slightly, catching herself, then continued toward the swing set, her steps slow.

"Ms. Maya." Jayden, his dark eyes serious behind his purple flexible glasses. "Ms. Diane didn't follow the path right."

"She's taking a break from games. You know, like you do sometimes."

"She got all sticky, though."

Oily, Maya would have called it. "That won't last," she said quietly, watching as Diane lowered herself heavily onto the bench by the swings, her hands trembling as she checked her phone. "See, it's already wearing off." But the weariness would remain.

All her thirty-nine years, she'd watched people walk through the floaters. Watched them grow more tired, more drained, more ill. Been told, again and again, it was all in her head.

She glanced down at Mitchell, still carefully following her path, still able to see what was really there. In no time at all, he would lose this skill, like all the others. The thought made her profoundly sad.

In the distance, the zigzag-tailed floater pulsed as if it breathed.

The dingy-white van had been parked across from Little Explorers Preschool for three days now. Maya had noticed it immediately—a stranger vehicle with government plates and a weathered logo she couldn't quite make out. She'd also noticed the gray-haired woman who sat inside, occasionally raising binoculars to her eyes.

Now, the woman finally emerged from the van. Dressed

too warmly for the weather in black slacks and a black blazer over a worn cornflower-blue blouse, she moved slowly, not avoiding the floater right by the van. Maya watched from the corner of her eye while supervising the climbing dome. It was too hot to climb much; the kids were mostly sitting on the crossbars swinging their legs.

The woman approached back gate of the playground fence, the one closest to the climbing dome. She waved to Randall, their forty-something janitor with the wide, open face. When he came close, she handed him a piece of paper, and then, after a bit, read it with him. He was a slow reader.

He nodded and smiled, and unlocked the gate. The woman made her way directly to the bench nearby, barely missing a floater hanging out beside the stained wood slats of its back.

"Hey, Di," Maya said. "I'm going to check on our visitor."

Diane waved acknowledgment while reminding Bailey to look where he was going.

Maya quickly positioned herself between the children and the stranger. Up close, she could see that the woman's hands trembled slightly, and thin white scars crisscrossed her fingers like a roadmap.

"Can I help you?" she asked. "Visitors need to check in at the office first."

The woman smiled, the corners of her eyes crinkling. "I did. Your director gave me written permission to observe. I'm Eleanor Vance, Western Division." She patted the bench beside her. "Would you mind sitting with me for a moment, Ms. Fane?"

Maya hesitated, then sat down, maintaining a professional distance. "Western Division?"

"Environmental Harmonics," Eleanor replied, her eyes not

on Maya but on the space on the other side of the climber—exactly where that zigzag floater pulsed and shimmered. "Tell me, how long have you been playing that game with the children? The one where you lead them away from danger?"

Maya stiffened. "It's just a follow-the-leader exercise. Kids enjoy movement games."

"Mmm," Eleanor said. "And it's just coincidence that your path carefully avoids this area?" She gestured toward the floater.

Maya's heart began to race. "I don't know what you mean."

Eleanor turned to face her fully. "I think you do, Ms. Fane. I think you've been seeing it for days. Maybe longer." She lowered her voice. "The crack forming right here. Or at least, what will become a crack."

"YOU... CAN SEE IT TOO?" Maya whispered, unable to hide her shock.

"Yes," Eleanor said. "It's just beginning to manifest in our dimension." She studied Maya's face. "I just happened to be driving by, and caught it early. It's not a danger, and I've had other things to handle. But you've been carefully guiding those children around it every day. You see it."

Maya swallowed hard. Thirty years of being dismissed, diagnosed, disbelieved—and now this stranger was talking straight out about the floaters as if they were real.

"I see them," she said.

"It's a dimensional crack," the woman said. She rubbed her scarred fingertips together. Her pinkie nail was black, even at the bed.

"Seriously?" Dimensional cracks had started to appear way back in the 1950s. A century and a half of industrial pollution and consumer plastics had weakened the wall between this reality and some other. A reality that was not safe for the beings of this world.

After the Cuyahoga River caught fire—again—in 1969, the problem became undeniable. People were fading— dying— and not just in cities. In the suburbs and small towns, in the shopping malls, in the places where industrial spew and consumer plastics met and mingled.

The government created the Environmental Protection Agency, charged with finding a way to combat this danger as well as other hazards. The way they'd come up with was magic. Supposedly. And to the "non-gifted," invisible.

When Maya was as little as Mitchell, the bright yellow vans of the Menders were all over the place. Wild-haired menders would arrive with a squeal of tires, rush into a parking lot, or beside a riverbank, or onto an airport's tarmac, wave their hands around, and rush out.

By the time Maya was in college, the Menders were a joke. What did they even do? The agency was halved, and halved again. Now Maya almost never saw a yellow van. The one Eleanor drove was so old it wasn't even yellow anymore, more like cream. Spoiled cream.

These days, everybody said these cracks were super rare. If they even existed. If they ever existed.

But floaters were all over the place.

"Our crew may be smaller than we once were," Eleanor said. "Victim of our own success, I suppose." She straightened her shoulders. Her suit coat was frayed at the collar. "But the work goes on. And my question for you is, why weren't you tested?"

In third or fourth grade, everyone got tested to see if they could hear well enough, read type without glasses, and see dimensional cracks. The tests were held in tents outdoors, since cracks never appeared indoors.

"I did get tested," Maya said. "The testers wanted me to point to one spot. I wasn't sure which spot they wanted." Not another joker, they'd said, dismissing her. "I didn't see anything that looked like cracks." In drawings, cracks looked like shadows of a child's drawing of lightning bolts, fat black or gray.

"Odd." Eleanor said. "But you see them now." She glanced at the children playing nearby. "You've kept them safe."

Relatively safe. Eliza and Ethan were racing each other up the climbing dome, their blond hair streaming behind them. Maya didn't dare call out and break their concentration. She held her breath instead.

Eliza touched the hexagon piece at the top of the dome first. Ethan slid down the pole attached to the center piece and got to the ground first. An argument began about where the race had officially ended. It quickly became screeching.

"We need you," Eleanor said. "We need more Menders."

"What?" Maya looked back to the woman beside her. She was wearing black running shoes. "Can't you just rehire folks?"

"We wear out." Eleanor rubbed her fingertips together again, this time looking down at them. "These last years, when a Mender retires, another is not hired. We've run through your generation—we thought—and since the mandatory testing was stopped after you, we don't have as big a pool to pick from." She smiled, more like a grimace. "We don't get a lot of volunteers."

"Liza!" Diane called out. "What did we say about pushing?"

Maya had to get back to work. Diane shouldn't have to watch everyone.

Maya stood up. "I already have a job. Like you say, keeping the children safe."

Eleanor pushed on the back seat of the bench to rise, her movements stiff. She handed Maya a plain white business card.

"Think about it overnight. I'll contact you tomorrow."

As Eleanor walked away, Maya looked down at the card. It contained only a name, "Western Division," and a phone number. No title, no agency logo.

She glanced out at the large floater with its zigzag tail, pulsing slightly. Growing.

"Ms. Maya!" Mitchell called from the sandbox. "Ms. Maya! Lookit my castle!"

AT SIX THE NEXT MORNING, Maya was peeling an orange while standing over the tiny sink in her apartment's efficiency kitchen when the email arrived with a happy bloop. The clear sky through her efficiency window promised another hot July day.

Maya wiped her hands on a dish towel before she tapped her phone screen to open the message.

And almost choked.

It was from Happy Toddler Daycare, Inc. The home office,

in Minneapolis.

Subject: Termination of Employment

Ms. Fane,

Following yesterday's official observation and multiple previous parent complaints, we write to inform you that your employment with our company is terminated, effective immediately…

The message continued with bureaucratic language about final paychecks and returning school property, and a PDF of the termination agreement for her to e-sign. Maya could hardly believe it. Parent complaints? There hadn't been any complaints—at least none she'd heard about. The children loved her games. They learned their letters, and about sharing. She doublechecked the sent from address; it was correct.

Her eyes drifted down to the second-to-last paragraph:

While we value creative approaches to early childhood education, your insistence on teaching children to avoid invisible "blobs" in the air has raised concerns about potential psychological impact. Several parents have expressed worry that their children now refuse to walk in straight lines, claiming they must avoid "jelly monsters" that will "make them tired."

She'd never said that. She'd been so, so careful not to say that. But kids were smart. They'd probably figured it out.

She'd led them right to it.

Four years of careful navigation, of protecting all these children without alarming them, of making safety into a game —this was how it ended. With the authorities dismissing everything she saw as delusion.

Again.

This was just like the Park Service job. And the parking lot attendant jobs. And the babysitting jobs.

All the jobs.

All her live-long days.

Twenty minutes later, she was still standing there, her butt against the sink counter, stunned, orange half-eaten, when her doorbell rang. Through the peephole, she saw Eleanor Vance standing in the plain white hallway. The Mender looked even more frail in the harsh fluorescent light. Her silver hair was neatly styled, but her hands trembled visibly as she adjusted her jacket. The same jacket as yesterday.

What a coincidence.

Maya hesitated, then opened the door. But she got the first word in.

"They fired me," she said flatly, before Eleanor could speak. "Email, just now. Apparently I'm filling children's heads with nonsense about floating oil spills."

Eleanor nodded, unsurprised.

"You did this!"

The woman had the gall to shrug. "The department does still have some sway. Would you take a ride with me?"

"No! Where are you taking me?"

"To the parking lot of the Northside shopping mall."

Maya frowned. "You mean Southside? The Northside one is shut down."

Eleanor's smile was small, and sad. "Come. Let us go see why."

MAYA WASN'T sure she should reward this job-stealing government lackey with another moment of her time. On the other hand, she didn't have anything else to do, apparently. She grabbed her phone and followed Eleanor down the bare second-floor apartment hall, down the unpainted cement stairs, and out into the heat.

Eleanor's van smelled like burnt coffee and wet socks, with an underlying metallic tang Maya couldn't place. The center console between the front bucket seats was cluttered with maps, crumpled fast-food bags, and two insulated drink cups with straws. A crystal pendulum hung from the rearview mirror, swinging erratically despite the smooth drive.

"Sorry about the mess," Eleanor said, easing the van onto the street. "And there's no AC, so you might want to roll down the window."

Maya shifted on the cracked vinyl seat, her hand coming away sticky from something spilled on the armrest. "Is this really a government vehicle?"

"You bet," Eleanor said, eyes on the road. "Repair, don't replace." She tapped a faded EPA sticker on the glove compartment. "The department keeps the lights on, barely."

"And these... dimensional cracks. They're really what I've been seeing all this time?"

Eleanor nodded.

Maya watched the city pass by in pure morning light. Factories and tall buildings and wooden homes and brick. Not a lot of people out yet. Floaters hovered over intersections, in parks, outside grocery stores. Had there always been so many?

"What exactly do Menders... do?" she asked.

Eleanor held her scarred right hand. "We mend. Seal the tears. It takes focus, training, and a certain innate ability. The kind you appear to have." She flexed her fingers. "It also takes a toll."

The van's CB radio suddenly crackled to life. Maya startled

—she'd thought the thing was an old-style radio, all knobs and buttons. Who even used CB radios anymore?

"Western Division. Class Emergence at Riverview Plaza on 23rd." The voice was tinny and distant. "Sounds like a Category three, already."

Eleanor sighed heavily, reaching for the handset, attached to the base by a twisty cord. She had to hold down a button on the side to talk. "This is Vance. Can someone else get this one?" She let go of the button and glanced at Maya apologetically.

Before they got a response, they reached the former Northside Mall. Eleanor pulled into the front parking lot, stopping just as the entry road hit the sea of empty parking spots. The huge lot—which once could hold a thousand cars and still need overflow parking during Christmas shopping—held none now. In the shade of the mall's main sign, on the grassy median between entry and exit roads, sat another beat-up formerly yellow van.

The mall, a two-story white cinderblock polygon, had a fancy open courtyard with a fountain in the middle that was a great spot to drink an Orange Julius and maybe flirt when she'd been a tween. Now all the mall's doors and windows were boarded up, lively store signs replaced by grimmer ones: black and white "No Trespassing." Red and yellow "Warning: Danger."

In the lot, wide swaths of the buckled concrete were overrun by plant life. Grasses as tall as her thighs. Stalks of Queen Anne's Lace that must be as high as her head. But plenty of bits of the huge lot were completely bare. Just the broken bits of road—and the floaters.

So floaters like to starve plants, too.

The radio crackled again. "Sorry, El. Nobody free. Peterson's crew is in Cincinnati, Rodriguez still on medical."

"Understood." Eleanor set the handset back in its cradle, her expression a mixture of irritation and weariness. She looked over at Maya. "I wanted to join you. Help explain. But now…"

"Is it always like this?" Maya asked. "Rush rush rush?"

"Some days it's worse. Rush rush, fail." Eleanor scared up a smile. She patted Maya's hand, avoiding the sticky part of the armrest. "But also, amazing."

"Still using that line, huh, Ms. Vance."

The cranky male voice at her elbow made Maya jump. She turned to find a young man—maybe early twenties—standing beside her door, just inches away from her elbow on the open window sill. Lean like he spent more time thinking than lifting. Short, dark hair dented along the middle like it was usually hidden under a baseball cap. Scowl that should be hidden under a cap. Black chinos and clean white t-shirt, black running shoes; must be Mender office style lite.

Arms crossed, weight shifted to one hip. In preschoolers, that pose signaled determinedly difficult. But his eyes held the shade of exhaustion Maya recognized from her own mirror. The kind that came from carrying responsibility you weren't quite ready for. Still, there was a challenge in his gaze, an intelligence that made her think he was probably very good at whatever he did.

"Maya, this is Jordan. He's our best teacher."

"If by best, you mean easiest to keep out of the field without mucking everything up." His voice didn't sound as grizzled as he probably thought it did. Too squeaky.

"Out you go." Eleanor tapped the lock button, and Maya's

door clicked. Jordan pressed the latch and pulled the door open, backing up as it swung toward him.

Maya stepped out of the van, and the heat slapped her like she'd stepped into a walk-in oven. The asphalt was already soft underfoot, and she could feel sweat beginning to gather behind her knees, at the small of her back, everywhere. There must be thousands of insects here, the buzz was so loud.

The van already was pulling away, turning to go back up the entry road and away. Eleanor's hand raised in what might have been apology or farewell. Gravel sprayed as she accelerated toward the street, leaving Maya standing alone with a stranger in an empty parking lot at six thirty in the morning.

Jordan kicked at a piece of broken concrete, frustration in every line of his body. Not cranky then. Maybe mad at being sidelined, stuck teaching instead of doing. But he should understand that training another Mender would mean one more person to help the next day.

Guess she'd decided to do this thing, then.

"Look, I'm sorry you got stuck with me," Maya said, "but I didn't ask for this either."

Jordan looked at her properly for the first time, taking in her pink capris, her big smock with multicolored ABCs printed all over it. His expression softened slightly.

"No, I'm sorry. It's just—" He gestured broadly at the empty lot. "We're barely keeping up as it is. Christof's has been out for three weeks with nerve damage in his hands. Eleanor's running herself ragged. And here I am, teaching basics instead of sealing cracks."

"How long have you been doing this?" Maya asked.

"Four months." He said it like a confession. "My mentor burned out in the spring. Literally—his hands started shaking so bad he couldn't seal anymore. So now I'm the experienced one." He laughed, but there was no humor in it. "Twenty-three years old and I'm training recruits."

Maya looked around the vast parking lot, really seeing it for the first time.

"So many," she breathed.

She looked back at Jordan. His hands were constantly moving—flexing, stretching, rubbing his palms against his jeans. The backs of his hands were smooth, unmarked, unlike Eleanor's. But when he turned them palm-up she caught a glimpse of deeper creases, lines that looked too pronounced for someone his age.

"Your hands," she said. "Are they…?"

"Occupational hazard." Jordan flexed his fingers again. "Every seal has to be precise. Perfect. Or it burns. The more you compress, the more chances to slip up."

He started to walk toward one of the open spaces, skirting a forest of weeds. Maya had to skip to keep up. A floater drifted past them, about head-height, one of the burnt sugar ones. Maya stepped aside automatically. Jordan went right under it.

He couldn't see it?

"Compress?" she asked.

"That's closing the seal by pressing your palms together. But you'll start with pinching." He stopped in the almost circular open space. "See something?"

She saw lots of things, including four floaters, the largest one maybe a hand's width. That's why the circle was so big, and not quite a circle.

"Which one?"

He looked at her like she had three heads. "The crack?"

Maya shook her head. "I don't see them as cracks. I see them as, sort of, blobs."

Jordan took that in, thought about it a moment, and then shook his head.

"Watch me." He stepped up to one of the floaters, the one with the tiny zig-zag tail. More like a zig-only tail. "See this?" He pointed to the floater.

"Yes."

"This one is small, so I'll use a pinch. Like this." He reached out, toward the little tail, and pinched it.

For a moment, the tail seemed to wriggle in his fingers. The muscles in his hand tensed, keeping hold of it. Then a pop, like your ears popping when a plane descends, and the tail was gone.

But the floater was still there.

"These are dimensional cracks. Holes in reality." Jordan's voice took on a lecturing tone, really annoying with that squeak in his voice. "We think it's another reality, but not one healthy for earth forms. The cracks suck energy from whatever they come near. Make some people sick, kill others instantly."

He pointed toward the mall entrance, a row of a dozen big pieces of plywood under a cement arch that used to be painted orange. "Eventually, if we don't get to them fast enough, they extend, and destabilize entire city blocks. Or malls."

"There's a crack over there?"

"You can't see it?" Jordan looked dumbfounded. "You've got to be kidding. It's taller than top of the mall."

"I don't see anything like that." The familiar frustration made her choke. Not believed, again. "I don't understand."

"No, it's me who doesn't understand." He looked at her,

looked at the mall entrance, looked at her again. "How can you see the tiny ones and not the gigantic ones?"

Maya shook her head. She picked up a foot, wiggled it slightly as if that would cool it off. Her feet were burning up even in her breathable espadrilles; Jordan's must be melting in those sneakers.

"I see floaters everywhere," she said. "All the time. But no cracks. Never."

"Floaters?" Jordan squinted his eyes almost shut. He frowned. Took a deep breath. "Whatever. Come on."

He walked past a patch of monster ragweed and the red-poison berries of pokeweed toward another bare circle about fifty feet away. "Let's try again."

This floater was smaller than the first, maybe the size of an see-through golf ball, but its zigzag tail had more kinks. Maya approached it cautiously.

"You see it, right? Let's you try." Jordan said, positioning himself beside her. "Pinch it at the top. If it needs more, we'll pinch it again at the next kink, and the next, until it pops. Pinch hard."

Maya reached out, thumb and forefinger extended. The tail felt like buzzing honey against her skin, sticky and wrong. "Here?" Jordan nodded. She pinched, as hard as she could.

The piece of gossamer and air bucked, and almost took the skin of her forefinger with it.

"Harder," Jordan said, his voice urgent. He put his hand around hers and added pressure to the pinch. "You're giving it energy. If you let go, it will be stronger and harder to pinch next time."

Maya squeezed until her fingertips went numb, until the muscles in her hand cramped. The tail writhed between her fingers, and something like electricity shot up her arm. Then—pop. The same ear-popping sensation as before.

The tail was gone. But the floater still bobbed in the air.

"Yeah!" Jordan said. "Clean seal, one pinch. How do you feel?"

Maya flexed her fingers, noting the lingering numbness. "Tingly. Tired." She looked at the floater. "But why don't we do anything about the rest of it?"

Jordan frowned. "The rest of what?"

"The floater. It's still there. Still…" Maya gestured vaguely. "Still doing whatever it does. Still draining energy from things."

Jordan looked at the spot where the crack had been. He squinted, hard. "How big is this thing you see?"

"This one's only as big as a golf ball. Sometimes it's an apple, sometimes a quarter, sometimes a dinner plate."

"And it's near where the crack was?"

"Not near. Attached." Maya rolled back on her heels to give her sizzling toes some air. "So it's only the ones with the zig-zag tails you're looking for."

Jordan went very still. "Wait. What do you mean, only those ones? How many of these floaters do you see?"

Maya wiped sweat out of her eyes. At least her hair was up and off her neck. Scrunchies were the best. Scrunchies on a summer's day.

She wasn't making sense.

"Can we go sit in the van a minute? I feel a little dizzy."

Jordan smacked his forehead. "Right. I forgot. Newbies need to eat after they practice." He took her hand, still tingly, and practically dragged her to the van.

Partially shaded by the mall's once-great main sign, the

van was relatively cool. Jordan pulled the side sliding door open and gestured for Maya to sit on the floor, her feet on the tall grass.

Men.

From the footwell of the front passenger seat, he pulled out a little white cooler with a square red top. He set it beside Maya. Inside among the refreezable icepacks were a six-pack of off-brand cola and a box of twelve plain donuts, ten left. Jordan took out two cans, and handed one to her. He let her choose her own donut.

They actually tasted good together, the cola acting as frosting for the only slightly less sweet donuts.

"Okay," Maya said after a bit, "help me understand. All you have to do, if you can see a crack, is pinch it closed? Push it hard?"

"Pretty much." Jordan cracked open a second can of cola. His poor stomach. "The little ones, like today, for sure. The bigger ones, you need better technique, and the willingness to potentially lose more than a little bit of yourself if you're not careful."

He grabbed another donut. Maya shuddered.

"More pop?"

"No, thank you. So it's just the seeing that's the problem?"

"I guess." Jordan shrugged. "But hardly anyone can see them."

The tiniest breeze wafted by. Maya prayed it hadn't wafted by the ragweed first.

So Jordan didn't see the floaters, but he did see cracks. She couldn't see cracks, but she could see floaters, some with little tails.

What if they were the same thing?

Maya gasped. The cola she'd just sipped started to go down the wrong way. She started to cough, hard.

"You okay?" Jordan came closer. He looked like he was thinking of slapping her on the back.

"Wait." She held up a hand, trying to cough herself back to normal. It took half a minute. "Listen. What if we're just using different words? You called it a tiny crack, where I called it a tail."

"Makes sense." Jordan stepped back, happily out of back-slapping range. "Of course you wouldn't have the right vocabulary for it."

"But." Maya's voice was getting faster now, trying to get the words to match the speed of her thoughts, trying to catch the idea before it wafted by. "What if the tail actually grew? What if the tail could become the crack?"

"Huh?" Jordan frowned, and then shoved half a donut in his mouth and grabbed another. "Tell me more about these floaters. You call them that because they're floating? They move?"

"Not really, I guess, a little? More because of what they look like. Those itty-bitty squiggle-blob thingies you get in your vision. You know? You see them in the corner of your eye, or when you stare at a white wall. But when you look at them, they seem to slide away. Eye doctors call them floaters."

"You spend a lot of time staring at white walls?"

"Ha ha. Look up, at the sky." It was more creamy blue than white, but still kind of like a blank wall. She looked up, modeling like for the kids. There were her familiar two floaters, on the right and up in the corner.

He looked up. But he was moving his head, like he was searching the sky.

"Stare at it." She used the Ms. Maya Means Business voice. "Fix on one spot."

Jordan actually did as she said.

The hand holding half a donut dropped to his side.

And then came up again.

He dropped his gaze and looked at her.

"I got nothing." He took a bite of his donut.

Maya glared at him before she could catch herself. Twenty-three years old. Probably didn't even have floaters yet.

She wished Eleanor had stayed.

"Okay, try this. Logic. First, let's say I do see these icepack thingies."

"If you say so." Jordan looked at the cooler. He could not possibly want more cola already.

"Second assumption: I can distinguish between two types of blobs, those without tails and those with tails."

He took out another can of cola. Maya shuddered.

"Third assumption: You don't see blobs, but you can see the tail part of the blobs that have tails."

"I'm not following."

"Listen, please. Ears open." Jordon snorted. "Sorry," Maya said. "Occupational hazard. But just consider: What if the blobs and the cracks are the same thing?"

"Yeah," he said, dismissing her. "So why can't we both see them?"

"I don't know. Different wavelengths?" Maya wiped sweat off her forehead. "Doesn't matter." She got up and started to pace, trying to stay in the shadow of the sign.

"What if, maybe, the tails eventually consume the floater part? And grow into full cracks. They take energy from us, but scaffolding or something from the floater?" She was walking too far: into the sun, back into shade, back into sun. "That's why I can't see big cracks. By the time they're that big, the original floater is gone. Consumed."

"Okay, so." Jordan rubbed his chin. "You're saying that something is here with us already before the crack appears. Like a larval stage?"

"Yes! Like a caterpillar, growing up into a butterfly."

"A life-sucking butterfly."

"Well, yes." She winced. "We try to make the metaphors positive at Happy Toddler."

"Hmmm." Jordan scanned the parking lot, with its dozens of small open spaces where nothing seemed to be, but nothing could grow. "So, a Category 1 crack is what you'd call a tail."

"What if sealing the tail stops the conversion? Or stalls it?"

Jordan rubbed at the bridge of his nose. "We leave those little cracks. We're swamped. They don't do much harm."

"But then do you have to come back, when they get bigger?"

His gaze snapped to her. "Maybe." His expression shifted like a child tasting her first SweeTart: confusion, anger, concentration, wonder. "We do see repeat cracks. By the river, here at the mall." He frowned at the mall as if its dull white cinderblocks offended him. "Not a lot, not always, but some, consistently. It's like those parts of the veil—dimensional curtain, whatever—is thinner."

"Or not."

"Or not." He tapped his lips, thinking. "So instead of getting panicked reports of Category 4 cracks and rushing around trying to close them, we could stop them when they're still larva. When they're easy to seal."

Then he sighed, defeated. "But nobody can see them."

Not quite. Maya stopped directly in front of him.

"We need you to see these floaters."

"Good luck with that." Jordan slumped against the van. He kicked up some dust. "We need to find more people like you. But how would we even test for that?"

He threw his hands up. "Put out an ad—'Hey, do you see squiggle thingies that aren't really there? Call the Menders.' People already think we're crazy. Or liars."

"How do you see cracks?"

"Theory is they are at the far edge of human visual spectrum. Right at the edge. So natural genetic distribution produces us outliers."

"I'm not an outlier."

"I don't know what you are."

Maya turned away from him. The jungle parking lot stood still, waiting for what wind would come. "I've seen them all my life. Some of my kids say they see them. There's plenty of us to help out."

What was different about the kids? Were their eyes rounder, or less round? The way they focused their eyes?

At the eye doctor's, what was the machine to look at floaters?

"Ophthalmoscope," she said.

"Ten-dollar word."

Maya pulled out her phone and searched the net. "Forced focal length change. Basically, bright light and a mirror." She looked around the parking lot, her gaze settling on the van. "What if we could recreate that effect?"

Jordan followed her gaze. "The side mirror?"

"And your phone's flashlight. If I'm right about how this works..." Maya was already walking toward the front of the van. She grabbed the side mirror, and twisted it to face the mall.

It broke off in her hand.

"Well," she said after a moment. "Now it's portable."

She went back to where Jordan was and faced the mall. She held the mirror at chest height.

"Okay. I'll shine my flashlight on here, and I'll move it slowly to try different angles. Try to look past the mirror, not at it. Through it? Look toward the mall, like you're trying to see something far away."

Jordan positioned himself as she directed. Maya angled the mirror to catch the morning sun, then pulled out her phone and turned on the flashlight, directing it to reflect off the mirror's surface.

"Now look through the reflected light. Let your eyes relax, like you're looking at one of those magic eye pictures."

For a moment, nothing happened. Then Jordan snapped to attention.

"Holy shit," he whispered. "They're everywhere."

She looked where he was staring. Three floaters drifted lazily in the space where they'd pinched off the tail, two more in the space beyond.

"The ones with the tails," he said, a little dazed. "Just… right here."

He shook his head, hard. "Gotta call Eleanor."

***

THEY MET at Happy Toddler at seven-thirty, just before it was due to open. Cars would be already lining up, ready to launch their little ones into the waiting arms of Diane and the others, so Maya told Eleanor to meet them by the back gate, by the climbing dome.

The playground looked smaller than Maya remembered, the poured rubber surface already radiating heat in the morning sun. Jordan parked his van in the same spot where Eleanor had sat watching her. A few minutes later, Eleanor parked right behind them. She met them at the gate.

"What's the emergency, Jordan?" Eleanor stopped, looked hard at Jordan. His pale face was splotchy, his breathing ragged, his hands clenched around the van's broken-off side mirror. "What happened to you?"

It didn't take a minute for Randall to see them. As he came closer, his smile was bright in his sunny round face.

"Maya not going to come around any more, Diane," he said. "But here is Maya." He looked at Eleanor, herself a little frazzled after slapping closed a Category 4 near the power station. "And a friend. And a new friend."

He unlocked the gate, and Maya, Eleanor, and Jordan passed through.

"Thank you, Randall," Maya said. She was going to miss him. "There," she said to the others, pointing to the center of the playground. "About five feet up. See it?"

"See what?" Eleanor said, walking toward it, looking this way and that. Jordan and Maya followed.

When they were only about six feet away, Maya put a hand on Eleanor's shoulder to stop her. "Try now," she said to Jordan.

Jordan stepped beside Eleanor and held up the broken side mirror, angling it to catch the sunlight. Maya shone her phone's flashlight toward the mirror, while Jordan tried different angles.

His expression shifted from concentration to alarm.

"Holy crap! That thing is huge." Jordan moved the mirror in front of Eleanor, trying to keep the angle the same. "Look through this light," he said. "Like you're looking out over the sea."

Eleanor looked, and frowned, and squinted. And failed.

"Nothing," she said.

Jordan didn't take that for an answer. He moved to stand right behind Eleanor, and hunched to get his head down to her height.

"I'm going to reach around you, okay?"

"Fine." Eleanor crossed her arms and sank down on one hip. "I have places to be."

Jordan held the mirror kitty-corner to both their gazes, and they tried again.

The moment Eleanor saw the floater she reared back, knocking Jordan so hard he lost his balance and hit the ground. "I lost it!" she said "Put it back!"

Jordan scrambled up. He hadn't let go of the mirror. This time, he stood beside Eleanor, and they found the right angle again.

"It's right there," Eleanor breathed. "Huge as life."

The floater had actually shrunk a little, down from a dinner plate to a tea saucer, but its zigzag tail now writhed. The air around it shimmered with a distortion that had nothing to do with the temperature.

"I noticed it changing a couple days ago," Maya said. It's must be getting ready to crack," Maya said. "I think."

They carefully stepped nearer. Up close, the floater was even more intimidating. Its iridescent twisted-string surfaces roiled. The familiar burnt sugar scent was now tinged with something bitter like tar. The zigzag tail almost touched the ground.

Eleanor looked at Jordan. "You seeing this?"

"Now I am," he said. "Couldn't even see the tail before. We think it's an earlier stage of cracking." Jordan winced, and looked an apology to Maya

"You mean," Eleanor said, "We stop it now, and maybe stop it forever?"

"That's Maya's theory," he said.

"Try," Eleanor said. "You two; I need to recover from the last one."

Jordan showed Eleanor how to hold the mirror, and then took Maya's hand.

"You lead?" he said. "We'll probably need to do three pinches. The kink at the tip first and on toward the body."

Maya's stomach clenched, but she nodded yes. The golf-ball-sized floater at the mall had left her fingertips numb for a few minutes. What would this one do?

This tail felt like grabbing an electric eel wrapped in cold honey. Maya's fingers immediately went numb, then began to burn as the thing fought her. Jordan's hands joined hers, adding his strength to the pinch.

"Hold on," he gritted out. "Don't let go."

The tail bucked and writhed, and Maya felt her energy draining away as if someone had pulled the plug on a bathtub. Her vision started to gray at the edges.

"Almost—" Jordan's voice was strained. "Almost—"

The smallest pop, and the first section of tail vanished.

Maya staggered backward, her hands shivering. But there were two more.

"Good," Jordan said. "Next one."

They worked their way back toward the floater's body, each pinch harder than the last, the tail growing thicker and more aggressive as they approached its source. After the second "pop," Maya's palms felt frozen and Jordan was swaying on his feet.

"Together," he said, and they both grabbed the base of the tail where it met the floater's body.

This time, the resistance was enormous. The tail whipped and twisted. She was being electrocuted. Her knees buckled. But Jordan's steady weight behind her kept her upright.

"Don't let go," he whispered. "Doing great."

The final pop was so loud it made her ears pinch. The massive tail vanished, leaving only the saucer-sized floater floating peacefully in front of them.

Maya collapsed onto the rubber surface, her whole body shaking. Jordan sank down beside her, his scarred palms pressed against his face. The tarry smell was lifting, leaving hot rubber, sidewalk crayon and donuts.

"Category 4," he said wonderingly. "Must have been. In larval stage. We just prevented a Category 4 crack."

Somebody started clapping, near the preschool building.

"You did it!" Randall said, his round face beaming. "Maya keeps the kiddos safe."

Jordan dropped his hands to stare at Randall. "You saw it?" he practically shouted.

Randall's smile vanished. "Um. Scary. Maya said don't go near."

"That's absolutely right, Randall," Maya said. She didn't remember saying that, but she couldn't be sure. The zig-zag electricity, or whatever it was, seemed to have shorted out parts of her brain.

Eleanor pivoted, looking around the rest of the playground.

"I see three more." She clicked off her phone flashlight and looked back at the climbing dome, with its floater just above like an iridescent crown. She sat cross-legged on the rubbery ground rather quickly. "I can still see it. Even without the mirror, I can still see it."

"Magic eye," Jordan said. "Remember those puzzles? Where there's a picture but you cross your eyes and you see a number."

"Magic eye," Eleanor repeated dreamily.

They sat there a minute or two, Eleanor looking bemused. Jordan rubbing his hands, watching Eleanor like he was waiting for something.

Eleanor went stiff.

"Shit," she said.

"Everyone can see them," Jordan said.

"And then they learn not to." Eleanor's voice grim with dawning realization. "We all did."

Jordan was quiet for a long moment, his hands still pressed against his knees. When he finally spoke, his voice was barely above a whisper. "How many?"

"What?" Eleanor asked.

"How many people did we dismiss in testing? How many 'jokers' who pointed to the wrong spot because they were seeing floaters instead of cracks?" His face had gone pale. "How many Randalls? How many Mayas?"

Eleanor's expression shifted from wonder to something much darker. She pulled out her phone, her scarred fingers fumbling with the screen. "Christof sealed forty-three Category 4s last year alone. Rodriguez, thirty-eight before his medical leave." She looked up at them. "If even half of those started as floaters that people could see…"

Maya watched the realization spread across their faces like a cherry sugar drink stain.

"Jesus." Jordan dropped his head into his hands.

"Language," Maya couldn't help saying. "Sorry."

"My mentor. He burned out sealing a Category 5 that had been growing for months in a strip mall. Months. If someone had called it in when it was still a baby…"

Eleanor stood up abruptly, then sat back down just as quickly. "How many communities have their own Maya?" she asked, staring at the climbing dome's floater. "How many could have had one but didn't? How many could have been calling in early warnings instead of waiting for cracks to tear open?"

Suddenly, noise exploded from the side door. First recess.

Not paying any heed to Ms. Diane calling after him, little Mitchell let go of his spot on the walking rope and barreled toward Maya. Jordan scrambled up to a stand, then helped Eleanor rise. But Maya waited for Mitchell.

"Ms. Maya! Ms. Maya!" His honey-graham-cereal hug hit her with the force of a Category 3 crack, but she held firm. "You didn't get to see us dance!"

"I'm so sorry, Mitchell. But I sure am glad to see you now."

"We have to tell them," Eleanor said to Jordan, looking down at Mitchell and Maya. "Tell them all."

Jordan sighed. "Tell them what, exactly? That the invisible things their kids have been seeing are real? That we've been wrong about everything?"

Eleanor's gaze moved across the playground. "That we need their help. That we always did."

Maya let Mitchell go. He zigzagged at top speed over to the climbing dome. Children ran across the playground, playing their games, avoiding the spaces where a floater drifted.

She felt something inside her smooth out, like rumpled paper being carefully flattened for a fresh drawing. These kids wouldn't grow up being told they were imagining things, making up stories, seeing what wasn't there.

No one would.

THE ARCHIVE OF ECHOES

MANDY HARPER'S fingers left smudges on the brittle page, tiny shadows against yellowed paper. Michigan State's main library's ancient heating system hissed and clanked in protest against the midwest winter, but even its aggressive warmth couldn't touch the furthest corners of the stacks. She'd been huddled here for—she glanced at the oversized number on her Casio watch—four hours and seventeen minutes.

"Shit," she said on a long exhale, the sound swallowed by rows of books stretching into dusk. Her muscles protested as she shifted position, high-waisted jeans digging into her stomach. She'd meant to take a break two hours ago.

Outside the library's Gothic windows, Reagan's America carried on with its big hair and bigger promises, the Challenger disaster still a fresh wound in the collective consciousness. In here, time moved differently—or hardly at all. That's why she came.

Why she stayed.

The familiar scent of dust and aging paper wrapped her

like a blanket. Comforting, constant. Unlike everything else in her life, books stayed exactly where you left them. They didn't drive off bridges on sleety winter nights.

Her eyes burned, vision blurring around the edges as she re-read the footnote that had consumed her afternoon:

For further discussion of the so-called "Library of Echoes," see Thornfield's "Apocryphal Collections and Literary Phantoms," now presumed lost.

Lost. Like so many things.

She'd checked all the special collections. Even asked the chief archivist, a cranky lady who did not like disorder.

The Smiths' live version of "There is a light that never goes out" played on repeat in her head as she traced the footnote with her fingernail. Professor Whitaker had dismissed her research proposal on apocryphal libraries as "charming but insubstantial," his condescension not-so-thinly veiled behind a paternal smile. He'd suggested a thesis on practical applications of regional folk medicines instead.

Practical. The word made her skin crawl. But she was here on a Barret scholarship, for local kids who'd had it tough, so she needed to toe the line.

Tomorrow.

Mandy tucked a strand of shoulder-length brown hair behind her ear, disturbing the mechanical pencil she'd forgotten was there. It clattered to the floor, the sound startling in the silence.

She should go. Take a break. The library was open all night; she could always come back. But she made no move to pack up the fortress of books surrounding her small pale oak corner carrel.

Instead, she reached for the next volume in her stack—a

weathered collection of Midwestern folklore she'd found misplaced in Medieval Studies. The spine cracked as she opened it, releasing a puff of old paper and binding glue, with faint notes of the rosemary oil Mandy dabbed on her wrists each morning.

She flipped through discolored pages, scanning chapter headings without much hope. This was the problem with chasing ghosts through footnotes. All you ended up with was paper cuts and disappointment.

Page 341 caught her attention. Someone had written in the margin—a cardinal sin in library etiquette. Normally, this would have irritated her, but the handwriting was so unusual —tiny, spidery and faded, yet precise—that she found herself leaning closer. Squinting.

Seek the door where the third squirrel perches, and speak the words: "Between the lines, beyond the pages."

Mandy frowned. The note had nothing to do with the text, which was discussing harvest rituals in southern Michigan. She flipped to the front of the book, checking the last date stamp: March 1967. Nearly twenty years since anyone had officially checked it out.

"Great," she said, stretching her arms overhead until her spine cracked satisfyingly. "Now I'm following the breadcrumbs of some flower child's research project."

But something about the note nagged at her.

The third squirrel.

She'd been practically living in the library since starting her graduate program two years ago, and she knew the building had its own squirrels—carved wooden ones, perched on the ends of the older bookshelves, the oaken stacks they'd had to tack to the walls when they started to list. The rodents were architectural flourishes from the original red-brick 1920s construction, before the unfortunate concrete additions of the 1970s.

Mandy chewed her lower lip, tasting waxy Chapstick. The sensible thing would be to pack up, go home to her cramped studio apartment, boil water for a ramen bowl, and start again fresh tomorrow.

Jack would have followed the note.

The thought snuck up, unbidden, unwelcome. Her brother had been gone for eight years now, but moments like this still ambushed her. Jack, seventeen forever, his room frozen in time at their parents' house. Posters of Led Zeppelin and Pink Floyd still taped to the walls, the friendship bracelet he'd made at summer camp still tied around her ankle.

"Fine," she said, as if he could hear her. "One quick look."

She gathered her notes into her canvas backpack, leaving the folklore book open on the desk. The library was nearly empty—a Thursday night in February didn't exactly draw crowds, and it was already past nine. The fluorescent lights buzzed overhead, casting everything in a sickly glow that made the '70s-era orange carpeting look particularly offensive.

Mandy remembered seeing a life-size carving of a squirrel on the third floor, in the northwest corner where the original architecture remained mostly untouched. She made her way there, boots silent on the carpet, the only sound the swish of her oversized Spartan-green sweater against her tan corduroy jacket.

The main lights had been dimmed in this section for the night. She had just enough to navigate by.

She found the first porcelain squirrel easily—a stern-looking porker, bushy tail high, guarding the entrance to Art

History. The model for this piece was probably great-great-granddad to the overfed crew who scurried around campus these days.

She moved deeper into the old stacks. The second squirrel, black with a smaller silhouette and skimpier tail, perched above Philosophy. Its wide round eyes seemed to follow her movement.

The third squirrel proved more elusive.

Mandy wandered through narrowing corridors of books, the shelves growing taller, the aisles tighter. This part of the library always reminded her of a labyrinth—rows and rows of knowledge arranged in perfect, bewildering order.

She loved it here, loved the logical chaos of it all.

But after fifteen minutes of wandering she was about to give up. Then she noticed a section of shelving that seemed different from the rest—darker wood, more ornate carvings. And there, on the shelf of a battered white oak bookshelf, perched the third squirrel. Smaller, sleeker, one of the rare red squirrels. Seeing one of these little guys on campus meant good luck. Unlike its wooden companions, this statue's eyes were closed, head tucked as if sleeping.

"Hiya," Mandy whispered.

She glanced around, suddenly self-conscious. The nearest study carrel was two stacks away. No one was watching.

Mandy cleared her throat, feeling ridiculous. But she said the words.

"Between the lines, beyond the pages."

Nothing happened.

Of course nothing happened. What had she expected? A secret passage to open? A ghostly apparition to appear?

She turned to leave, irritated with herself for indulging this wild goose chase, when a soft sound made her pause. Like pages turning, or a startled gasp.

She turned back.

The squirrel's eyes were open.

Mandy froze. Wooden squirrels didn't open their eyes. She was hallucinating. Too much caffeine and too little sleep.

But no—the carved squirrel definitely had open eyes now, gleaming amber in the dim light. And beside it, a seam had appeared between the bookshelves where no seam had been before, outlining a skinny door.

Mandy took a step back. She pulled her arms inside her oversized sweater and hugged herself. "Impossible," she said, loud, as if making doubtful noise would make the door disappear.

Instead, it swung inward, with the just the hint of a creak.

She had to slip in sideways.

Beyond the door lay darkness, silence that seemed to make a sound. The air that wafted out smelled ancient, like the pages of an illuminated book no one had opened in centuries.

Every rational neuron in Mandy's brain screamed at her to back away, to pretend she'd never seen this impossible door with its impossible rodent guardian. To go home, call her therapist, get more sleep.

But grief had hollowed places inside her that reason couldn't reach. For eight years, she'd been searching for answers. First in tear-soaked journals hidden under her mattress. Then in university psychology courses that dissected grief into sterile stages and processes. Now in these dusty books and forgotten lore.

What if the answers had been waiting for her all along, just beyond this threshold?

What if this was just another one of those weird utility closets, tucked into one of the library's many odd corners, and she was just being a ditz.

Mandy hesitated for one last moment.

Nope. She had to know.

She pulled her arms back into the sleeves of her sweater, took a deep breath, tightened her grip on her backpack strap, and stepped through the doorway.

Behind her, the squirrel's wooden eyes drifted closed once more, and the door whispered shut. She didn't hear it lock. She hoped.

PALE LIGHT CAME up like the dawn, sweeping the shadows from the floor to the ceiling.

Mandy's first thought: wow, it's bigger on the inside.

Her second: that's impossible.

The space stretched before her, vast and contradictory. Rows of oddly angled bookshelves extended into impossible distance, their tops lost in the shadows.

"Okaaaay," she said, her voice thin in the musty air.

She took a tentative step forward, the worn soles of her boots connecting with floor that wasn't linoleum or carpet, but something that felt like living wood. It yielded slightly beneath her weight, then settled. Mandy gasped, jerking her foot up. She wobbled for a couple of seconds, and then cautiously replaced it.

"Hello?" She called out. Her voice fell flat, absorbed by the surrounding books. No echo.

As her eyes adjusted to the dimness, she noticed ornate wooden supports carved to resemble tree branches. Tiny squirrel figures appeared to be climbing or watching, their wooden eyes following her movements. Mandy reached out to touch one, and it blinked. She yanked her hand back.

Some shelves ended in delicately carved squirrel tails that curled around corners, while reading alcoves were marked by squirrels in different poses—gathering knowledge rather than nuts, she thought with unexpected fondness. Hadn't squirrels been treated as pets back when this part of the library was built?

The nearest bookshelf seemed to call to her, not with sound but with feeling. A magnetic pull that urged her closer. She stepped toward it, the living floor creaking beneath her. Unlike the metal or hardwood shelving of the other library, these were carved from some dark wood she couldn't identify, polished to a gleam that winked in the light.

Mandy ran her fingertips along the shelf's edge, surprised by its warmth. The wood seemed to respond to her touch, a subtle vibration traveling up her arm.

"Okay, Mandy," she said to herself. "Either you're having the most vivid hallucination of your life, or…"

Or what? She'd discovered a secret library hidden within MSU's main branch? A magical realm accessed through a door guarded by an animated squirrel carving?

Jack would have loved this.

The thought brought equal measures of comfort and pain. She could almost hear his voice: "Holy shit, Mand! This is like something straight out of D&D!"

She hadn't been allowed to play the game with his friends, being a cootie-filled fourteen-year-old girl. But Jack let her help plot out the story, the traps, and the prizes.

As she passed the first set of shelves, a book to her left

shifted slightly, edging out from its perfectly aligned neighbors. Mandy didn't even startle. Nothing could surprise her in this place.

The book was thin, bound in dark green leather with no title on its spine. Without conscious decision, Mandy reached for it. The leather felt warm beneath her fingers, like skin that had just been touched.

"I wouldn't do that if I were you."

The voice was neither high nor deep, but melodious, the words precisely enunciated. Like someone who had learned English from books rather than conversation.

Mandy yelped, spinning around so quickly she nearly toppled over. The books in her backpack slid hard to the side, punching her in the ribs.

A medium-sized person-shaped figure stood at the end of the aisle. Tall, silver-haired, with skin so dark it seemed to have its own luminescence. Impossible to tell if the person was old or young, male or female. They wore what looked like a charcoal gray suit that moved in ways fabric shouldn't, as though responding to air currents Mandy couldn't feel.

"Hello," she said, sounding braver than she felt. Her heart drummed a wild rhythm against her ribs. "What is this place?"

The figure glided toward her—not walking, exactly, but moving with unnatural smoothness.

"I am the Keeper of this collection. You may call me the Librarian. And this," they gestured with long, elegant fingers, "is the Library of Echoes. Though some call it the Phantom Archive."

Mandy stumbled back slightly as a book on a nearby shelf fluttered its pages. "Names are slippery things here, aren't they?" she said, trying to maintain some semblance of academic detachment.

"Indeed." The Librarian's mouth curled in what might have been appreciation.

"You're not real," Mandy said, steadying herself against a shelf that seemed to lean into her touch like a cat. "I'm hallucinating. Or dreaming. Or—"

"You're experiencing a reality that exists alongside your own," the Librarian interrupted.

A rustling sound spread through the library—pages turning, paper shifting. Mandy spun around, watching as books throughout the vast space seemed to stir.

"What is it?" she asked, backing toward the door she'd entered through. The door that was now closed.

"They're curious about you," the Librarian said. "New readers are rare."

Mandy glanced at a nearby shelf where a small carved squirrel perched, its wooden eyes somehow alert and watchful. "What about these little guys? They don't seem like ordinary decorations."

The Librarian followed her gaze. "Our guardians. They have been with us since the beginning."

"Guardians? But they're just carvings," Mandy said, though she didn't entirely believe it.

"Squirrels have been gathering and preserving knowledge since long before humans built their first libraries," the Librarian said, moving to stand beside her. "They collect fragments of the world and hide them away safely. Caches, that sustain through seasons of scarcity."

Mandy reached out, hesitantly stroking a wooden squirrel's tail. It vibrated under her touch. "So they're... alive?"

"They move easily between worlds. Ground and sky, visible and hidden. Rather like this library itself."

As if to emphasize the point, the rustling sound intensified, rising from whisper to murmur. Mandy could have sworn she heard voices within it, fragments of conversations long past.

"The books," the Librarian said. "Words written with conviction or passion or desperate need leave... imprints. Echoes."

Mandy found herself drawn back to the green book, her fingers hovering near its spine. A magnetic pull she couldn't resist.

"Volumes here tend to call to the readers who need them most." The Librarian glided closer, to read the spine of the book. Nothing was written on the spine, but the Librarian seemed to recognize it anyway. Their gaze grew sharper. "But need and want aren't always aligned."

Mandy's academy-trained skepticism battled with the evidence of her senses. There was only one question she wanted the answer to. Did this book contain it? How could it possibly?

Her fingers inched closer to the green spine. "What will happen if I read it?"

"Knowledge changes you. You know that." The air around Librarian was chill, as if they were made of ice. "But here, the effect is more immediate. More profound."

A shiver ran down Mandy's spine. "Could it hurt me?"

"That depends on what you consider harm." The Librarian circled her slowly. "What would you say causes more pain— knowing a difficult truth or forever wondering what might have been?"

Mandy considered this, her hand still hovering near the

book. It had been eight impossible years. She was ready for the truth.

The Librarian was close enough now that Mandy could see their eyes—pale, not a single color but shifting, like pages being turned. "These books contain the unedited fabric of reality—truths that have been written and erased, futures that were imagined but never came to pass."

What?

"They show the past? As it really happened?" Mandy's voice dropped to a whisper.

"Perhaps. Or they can show you what might have been." The Librarian paused, studying her reaction. "They can even, in rare cases, rewrite what was."

Mandy's breath caught. She touched her throat, restarting her heart. "Rewrite the past?"

"Take care, Amanda Harper." The Librarian's voice sharpened. "Many have entered this library seeking to change what cannot be changed. None have left satisfied."

Many stepped back, suddenly chilled to the bone. "How do you know my name?"

"The library knows all who enter. It reads you as surely as you would read it."

The green book shifted again, almost imperceptibly. Was it humming? Mandy's fingers tingled with the need to touch it, open it, let it loose.

"You've been searching for something," the Librarian said, looking away from her, toward the shadowed stacks in the distance. "Not for academic glory or intellectual curiosity."

Mandy swallowed hard, tasting copper. "My research—"

"Is a shield, not a purpose." The Librarian's gaze seemed to pierce through her hard-scabbed defenses. "That is not why you are here, Amanda Harper."

Mandy swallowed thick, her mouth dry as paper and paste. "I don't know what you're talking about."

The Librarian gestured toward the green book. "See."

Finally. Mandy reached for the book. It slid from the shelf into her hand, eager to be held. The faux-leather was supple, the stitched binding perfectly fitted to her palm. A book well-read, well-loved.

She opened it slowly, carefully. Trying to tamp down her expectations. Her fears.

The first page was blank except for a single line in a familiar, sloppy hand:

Property of John "Jack" Harper, 1977—

Her brother's last journal. The one that had gone missing after the accident. The one she'd torn his room apart looking for, convinced it held some explanation, some final message.

Impossible. "This was lost years ago," she said.

"Nothing written is ever truly lost," the Librarian said. "All words leave echoes. Some louder than others."

Maybe the book had escaped to this library. Maybe the squirrels had stolen it. Maybe it was a copy.

Maybe it was a lie.

Mandy's hands trembled as she turned to the next page. Jack's handwriting filled it, the entries dated. Ragging about about school, gossiping about friends, copying song lyrics. She flipped through, watching his life unfold on the pages. A fight with their dad. The time he got suspended for skipping class to see a Yes concert. "Worth it," he'd written.

A first kiss—Artemis, she knew it!—and then more salacious details. Mandy started to skim, then just flip pages.

The writing ended just past the middle of the journal. She turned back ten pages, a long two weeks before the end.

The entries had grown darker. Jack felt trapped, pressured to be "the good son," whatever that meant. No one understood. The pills he'd started taking from their mother's medicine cabinet were losing their effect. He had to take more to find that "comfortably numb."

Mandy's chest tightened. "He never said anything," she said, her voice small. "I didn't see it."

"Brothers protect their sisters," the Librarian said. "Even from the truth."

The last entry was dated October 3, 1978—three days before the accident. Jack and their father had yet another big blowout. Dad said Jack would never measure up, and in the journal, Jack agreed. He was tired of pretending.

The final line made her breath catch:

Sometimes I think about just driving away and never coming back. Just me and the big green Cutlass, hitting the road until we run out of gas or luck or whatever comes first.

Mandy closed the book, pressing it between her palms.

"Are you saying… it wasn't an accident? That he…"

The Librarian's expression remained neutral. "The book shows only what was written. What happened after is known only to him."

"But I could find out," Mandy said, realization dawning. "You said the books show what might have been. What if there's a book that shows what really happened that night?"

Around them, the library seemed to respond to her rising emotion. Books rustled on their shelves, the sound like nervous chittering. The floor beneath her feet grew warmer.

"You could," the Librarian said. "But some truths, once known, cannot be unknown."

How would that be a bad thing? Eight years of grief had hardened into determination. "I understand," she said.

The Librarian studied her, those page-turning eyes unreadable.

"This way."

They moved deeper into the archive, past shelves that seemed to branch and rearrange themselves as they approached. The air grew heavier, charged with something that made the hair on Mandy's arms stand on end. The rustling whispers and chitters of the books followed them, rising and falling like breath.

The corridor opened into a wide room, its high ceiling hidden in dimness. The branching bookshelves here curved with the walls and over the single doorway they'd entered through, creating a perfect circle. At the center stood a small reading desk and chair, both carved from the same dark wood as the shelves. A small green-glass shaded lamp cast pale light over the desktop.

"This section contains personal histories," the Librarian said. "Lives as they were lived, as they might have been lived, as they were thought to have been lived."

They gestured at the chair. "Sit. Think of your brother—not as you remember him, but as he truly was."

Mandy settled into the chair, surprisingly comfortable despite its lack of padding. She set her hands on the desk and closed her eyes, picturing Jack. Not the sanitized version their parents had constructed after his death—honor student, athlete, perfect son—but the real Jack. The one who'd taught her to play poker using Skittles as chips. Who'd snuck out to concerts and come home smelling of cigarettes and pot. Who'd cried watching "E.T." but sworn her to secrecy afterward.

Jack, who'd worn a Led Zeppelin T-shirt so often it had holes at the armpits. Jack, who'd made her a friendship bracelet at summer camp the year before he died, and then called her a total dweeb for wearing it—even as he'd kept his own tied around his wrist until the threads frayed.

A warm heaviness spread across her palms. Mandy opened her eyes to find a book had materialized on the desk before her. Thick, bound in worn brown leather with a yellow metal clasp, it had no title on its cover or spine.

She looked up, at the Librarian, who had not moved from the doorway.

"Your brother's complete history," the Librarian said. "Everything that was, everything that might have been."

Mandy reached for the first clasp with trembling fingers.

"Before you open that," the Librarian said, "understand what you hold. This isn't just a record—it's a potential. The books here don't just tell stories; they contain realities. To change what is written is to change what was lived."

Her hand pulled away from the clasp as if it was molten. "You mean I could change what happened to him?"

The air in the library grew suddenly cold, books shuddering on their shelves. The Librarian's frowned.

"That is neither wise nor permitted. The consequences of such actions reach far beyond your own meager lives."

But already Mandy's mind raced with possibilities. If she could rewrite the night of the accident—just a small change, moving the time forward or backward, altering the conditions —Jack might still be alive. Her parents might not have shattered into the brittle, distant people they'd become. Her own life wouldn't be defined by the abyss at its center.

"What's the point of having this power if you don't use it?" she said.

"Knowledge and power are not the same," the Librarian said. "This library preserves; it does not amend."

But the book beneath Mandy's hands seemed to pulse with possibility, calling to those open wounds within her.

"I just want to understand," she said softly, not entirely sure if she was lying. "Please."

The Librarian studied her, those shifting eyes unreadable. Finally, they nodded once. They stepped backward, through the doorway, seeming to dissolve into the shadows between bookshelves. Mandy was alone with her brother's book, the heat, the cold, the weight of its potential buzzing in the air around her.

She opened the clasp with a soft click and turned to the final pages. If she was going to find answers, they would be at the end—in the record of that rain-slick October night when Jack had taken the Cutlass out and never come back.

The pages seemed to turn themselves, stopping at October 6, 1978. There, in crystalline detail, was the account of her brother's final hours.

That last fight with their dad had been worse than anyone knew. Accusations hurled like weapons. About Jack's slipping grades. About the pills found in his jacket pocket. About the disappointment he'd become. Jack, seventeen and drowning, had grabbed the car keys and stormed out, their father's words chasing him: "You keep this up, you'll end up dead before you're twenty!"

Mandy read with growing horror as Jack drove aimlessly

for hours, as the thunderstorm blew in, as the windshield wipers started to struggle against the downpour. Saw through the book's unflinching gaze as he swallowed two of their mother's Valium, then two more. Watched as he turned onto River Road—a dangerous stretch even in good weather, with its sharp curves following the Red Cedar River's path.

The time was recorded with terrible precision: 11:47 pm. The Cutlass took the curve too fast. Jack, his reactions dulled by pills and anger and the rain streaming down the windshield, didn't brake in time, didn't turn the wheel. The car crashed took out the guardrail and plunged into the swollen river below.

The book detailed everything—the impact, the frigid water rushing in, Jack's final moments of clarity as the rain broke and he could see, could realize what was happening. His last thought: *I want to go home.*

Not suicide, then. Not intentional. But not purely accidental either. A terrible convergence of choices and circumstances that had ended with her brother trapped in a sinking car.

Mandy closed the book, hot tears drying cool on her face. So now she knew. She didn't feel any better. No comfort, no closure—only the sickening certainty that tiny changes might have saved him. If their father had listened as well as yelled. If Jack hadn't taken those pills. If he'd been on that road just three minutes later, and not already in the water, when the rain had started to slacken.

Three minutes.

The thought lodged in her mind like a splinter. Three minutes would have made all the difference. Three minutes was nothing—a song on the radio, a quick phone call, a couple of extra stop lights.

She reopened the book, turning to that fatal page. The time stared back at her: 11:47 pm. What if it had been 11:50? What if Jack had hesitated just a little longer before grabbing those keys?

Around her, the library seemed to hold its breath. The whispers ceased. Even the air grew still. Waiting.

Such a little thing.

She reached into her backpack, fishing for a pen. When her fingers closed around one—a blue Bic, chewed at the cap—she hardly hesitated.

A part of her knew this was wrong. Maybe even dangerous. But grief has its own gravity, its own spin. No way she wasn't going to do this. No way she wasn't going to try.

With surprisingly steady hands, she drew a line through "11:47" and wrote above it, in her neatest handwriting: "11:50."

For a moment, nothing happened. The ink glistened on the page, blue, wet, and ordinary. Mandy almost laughed at herself —what had she expected? Her brother to materialize beside her? The past to rewrite itself with a stroke of a drugstore pen?

Then she felt it—a tremor beneath her feet, subtle at first, then unmistakable. The floor seemed to breathe, rising and falling like a chest in distress. Around her, books began to slide from their shelves, thudding against the floor with sounds like distant thunder.

The air thickened, pressure building in her ears until they popped. The lamp on the desk flickered, its golden glow stuttering into darkness before flaring back to life.

And the book—Jack's book—grew warm beneath her fingers. No, not warm. Hot. Burning. The pages began to turn of their own accord, flipping backward, forward, settling, then flipping again, as if the book itself couldn't decide which version of reality to display.

The pain in her fingertips finally forced Mandy to snatch her hands away. She stood, knocking over the chair, backing away from the desk as the book continued its frantic dance. The leather binding began to smoke, curling at the edges.

"What have you done?"

The Librarian materialized beside her, those page-turning eyes now a storm of fury. They grabbed Mandy's arm, fingers bitingly cold through the fabric of her sweater.

"I just changed the time," she stammered. "Three minutes."

"Time!" The Librarian's voice resonated through the trembling room. "You have torn the fabric of what was. Created a paradox. Time doesn't exist in isolation, Amanda Harper. It's a tapestry, every thread connected to countless others."

Around them, the library's convulsions intensified. Books flew from shelves now, their pages fluttering like panicked birds. The walls themselves seemed to ripple, stretching and contracting in nauseating waves.

"What's happening?" Mandy had to shout over the cacophony.

"Reality's unraveling," the Librarian answered, their voice somehow cutting through the chaos. "You've created a fracture—a version of events that contradicts what was. The library is trying to reconcile the irreconcilable."

Mandy's stomach lurched as the floor beneath her feet

pitched sideways. She grabbed the edge of the desk to steady herself, her thoughts racing. "How do we fix it?"

The Librarian's laugh was bitter. "We? You altered what cannot be altered. You—"

A deafening crack cut them off. Above them, the ceiling split open, revealing not the floor above but a swirling vortex of words and images—fragments of stories, pages, lives being torn apart and reassembled.

"The book," the Librarian shouted, pointing to Jack's volume, which now lay open on the floor, its pages blackened at the edges. "You must restore what you changed."

Mandy dropped to her knees, reaching for the book. The heat radiating from it singed her eyebrows, but she forced herself to grab it, to find the page she'd altered.

There it was—her neat handwriting already fading, the ink bleeding into the page as if the book itself were rejecting the change.

"I need a pen," she gasped, patting her pockets frantically.

The Librarian pressed something into her hand—not a pen but a slender silver object that looked like a letter opener. "Use this. Your blood will seal the restoration."

Mandy didn't hesitate. She pressed the sharp tip to her finger, wincing as it broke the skin. A drop of blood welled up, startlingly bright against her pale skin.

"Now write the truth," the Librarian commanded. "Not what you wish had happened, but what did happen."

With shaking fingers, Mandy smeared her blood over the "11:50," watching as it disappeared beneath the brick-red streak. Then, using the silver instrument like a pen, she rewrote the original time: "11:47."

The blood sank into the page, disappearing as if absorbed

by a sponge. For a terrible moment, nothing changed—the library continued to tear itself apart around them, books and shelves collapsing into the growing vortex above.

Then, gradually, the tremors subsided. The books stopped flying, the walls ceased their undulating. The rip in the ceiling began to close, the swirling chaos beyond it receding like a tide.

Mandy sat back on her heels, exhausted. The book before her had returned to normal—the pages white, the leather binding intact. As if nothing had happened at all.

"What have I done?" she whispered, the full weight of her actions crushing down upon her.

The Librarian stood over her, their expression unreadable. "You've learned what many before you have learned, at great cost. The past cannot be changed, not even by the Library of Echoes. It can only be understood."

Mandy looked up at them, tears streaming down her face. "But what's the point of understanding if it doesn't change anything? If Jack is still dead?"

"Understanding changes everything," the Librarian said softly. "Not the facts, perhaps, but the meaning we give them. That is the true power of this place."

They extended a hand, helping Mandy to her feet. The library around them had grown quiet, the books settled back into their proper places. Only the scattered volumes on the floor remained as evidence of the chaos that had just subsided.

"So that's it?" Mandy asked, her voice hollow. "I just go back to my life, knowing what I know now?"

"What you do with knowledge is your choice," the Librarian replied. "But remember—the answer to grief is not to erase it, but to carry it differently."

Mandy looked down at Jack's book, still open on the floor. She knelt and picked it up, cradling it in her hands. "Can I… can I read the rest of it? Not to change anything, just to understand?"

The Librarian hesitated, then nodded. "The reading room is through there." They gestured to a door that Mandy was certain hadn't been there before. "You have until dawn. Then you must return to your world."

Mandy clutched the book to her chest, feeling its warmth—not burning now, but alive with memory. "Thank you."

As she moved toward the door, the Librarian's voice followed her: "Remember, Amanda Harper. The greatest magic is not in changing what was, but in transforming what is."

THE READING ROOM felt like a sanctuary after the chaos she'd just survived. Circular, like the room with the desk, but smaller and more intimate. A single armchair upholstered in worn velvet occupied the center, a floor lamp casting a gentle pool of light beside it. The walls here held no books, only tapestries in deep jewel tones depicting scenes Mandy couldn't quite make sense of—figures that seemed to shift when she wasn't looking directly at them.

She sank into the chair, its cushions conforming to her body as if they'd been waiting for her. Jack's book rested heavy in her lap. She'd nearly destroyed reality trying to change five minutes of his life. Now she just wanted to know him—truly know him, not the sanitized version their parents had constructed after his death, or even the idealized big brother she'd preserved in her memory.

Mandy took a deep breath, inhaling the scent of old leather and something else—the faintest hint of Drakkar Noir, the cologne Jack had practically bathed in during his final year. The memory was so visceral she glanced around, half-expecting to see him lounging against the wall, smirking at her.

She opened the book again, this time to the beginning.

John Michael Harper, born April 12, 1960.

What followed wasn't just dates and events, but thoughts, feelings, sensations—Jack's life rendered in exquisite, some-times painful detail. She read about his first steps, his first words ("No!"—some things never changed), the day he'd discovered their father's record collection and fallen in love with music.

She read about herself through his eyes—his fierce protec-tiveness, his genuine admiration for her intelligence, his guilt at teasing her so mercilessly about the fantasy novels she devoured. The way he secretly thought of her as the strongest person in their family, even when she was just a skinny twelve-year-old with braces and a vocabulary that intimidated his friends.

Hours melted away as she turned the pages. She laughed at memories she'd forgotten—the time they'd tried to camp in the backyard but ran inside at midnight, convinced they'd heard a bear (it was the neighbor's Saint Bernard). She cried reading about the day he'd found their mother passed out on the bath-room floor, vodka disguised in a mouthwash bottle beside her —a secret he'd kept from Mandy, cleaning up their mom and putting her to bed before Mandy got home from swim practice.

The Jack that emerged from these pages was more

complex, more troubled, and more remarkable than she'd imagined. A boy shouldering burdens too heavy for his age. A teenager fighting depression with whatever numbing agents he could find—alcohol, pills, the deafening wall of sound at rock concerts.

But not suicidal. Never that. Even in his darkest moments, Jack had clung to life with a desperate, defiant grip. What had happened that night had been a terrible convergence of anger, impaired judgment, and bad weather—not a deliberate choice to end his life.

When she finally reached those last pages again—the account of that final drive—she read them differently. Not looking for something to change, but for something to understand.

Their father's cutting words. Jack's reckless decision to drive while impaired. The rain-slick curve of River Road. The moment when he realized, too late, that he'd taken the turn too fast.

I want to go home.

The words still throttled her heart. But now they were just the truth—painful, unchangeable, but finally clear. Jack hadn't wanted to die. He'd made mistakes. Who hasn't? The tragedy wasn't that he'd chosen death, but that he'd lost the chance to grow beyond that night, to become the person he might have been.

Mandy closed the book gently. Against all odds, she felt something like peace settling into those jagged spaces inside her. Not filling them completely—grief didn't work that way —but lining them with understanding, making them less sharp, less empty.

She must have dozed off, because when she blinked awake, the Librarian stood before her, those shifting eyes solemn.

"It's nearly dawn," they said. "You must return."

Mandy nodded, wiping her cheeks. "The book—"

"Belongs here," the Librarian finished, holding out their hands.

She hesitated, clutching Jack's book to her chest. "I'll never see it again."

"No," the Librarian agreed. "But you've read what you needed to read. You carry it now, in ways that matter more than paper and ink."

Reluctantly, Mandy surrendered the book. Their fingers brushed as the Librarian took it, and she felt a jolt of something—not quite electricity, but a connection, as if for the briefest moment she glimpsed what the Librarian truly was. Not human, certainly, but not entirely otherworldly either. Something in between, like the library itself.

"Thank you," she said. The words felt inadequate for what she'd experienced, for what she'd learned, but they were all she had.

The Librarian inclined their head slightly. "The door that brought you will take you back. But be warned—the threshold between your world and this one can only be crossed a finite number of times by any mortal. The squirrel may not acknowledge you again."

"So I can never return?" The thought brought a surprising pang of loss.

"I didn't say that." The Librarian's almost-smile flickered. "Only that the way you came may not open for you again. There are other doors, other guardians."

They gestured toward an archway that had appeared in the

wall. Beyond it, Mandy could see the circular room with the desk, and beyond that, the endless rows of shelves that would lead her back to the door guarded by the squirrel.

"Wait," she said, a final question surfacing. "Why did the library reveal itself to me now? After all these years?"

The Librarian considered her, those page-turning eyes flickering with what might have been compassion. "Perhaps you weren't ready before. Or perhaps the library wasn't ready for you."

"That's not really an answer."

"No," they agreed. "But it's the one I have to offer."

Mandy could only nod. She rose from the chair, stretching muscles stiff from hours of reading. Her watch had stopped—she had no idea how long she'd been in the Phantom Library.

"Goodbye," she said, moving toward the archway.

"Remember what you have learned here." The Librarian's expression softened fractionally. "Next time, the library might not be so forgiving."

With that warning echoing in her mind, Mandy stepped through the archway. The reading room disappeared behind her, the tapestries and velvet chair fading like a dream upon waking. She made her way through the circular room, past the desk where she'd nearly unraveled reality, and into the endless rows of bookshelves.

The archive seemed different now—less threatening, more melancholy. Books softly chittered as she passed, not in alarm but in recognition. The floor yielded gently beneath her boots, guiding her steps rather than hindering them.

When she reached the small door, it opened at her approach. The carved red squirrel perched above it watched her with its amber eyes, unblinking. Mandy gave it a small nod, a gesture of respect and gratitude, before ducking through the opening.

The transition was jarring—from the ancient, living air of the Phantom Library to the sterile, processed atmosphere of the university building. Mandy stumbled slightly as she emerged, her body adjusting to the change. Behind her, the door swung closed with a soft click, the seam disappearing back into the ordinary bookshelf.

The regular library looked exactly as she'd left it—dimly lit, deserted at this late hour. But something had changed. Not the building, but her perception of it. The books around her now seemed faintly alive in ways she'd never noticed before—the whisper of pages shifting, the subtle vibration of knowledge contained within their bindings.

Or maybe she was the one who had changed.

Mandy made her way back to her desk, where her extra research materials still lay scattered exactly as she'd left them. The folklore book remained open to page 341, showing that cryptic marginal note. She ran her fingers over the spidery handwriting.

Who had written it? Another lost soul seeking answers? The Librarian themselves, reaching across dimensions to those who needed the library most? She supposed it didn't matter now.

What mattered was what she'd found there—not a way to change the past, but a way to understand it. To carry her grief differently, as the Librarian had said.

She gathered all her materials, cramming them into her backpack with new purpose. Her thesis on apocryphal libraries suddenly felt urgent in ways it hadn't before—not just an academic exercise, but a map to understanding how stories preserved truths that history often overlooked.

As she zipped her backpack closed, the fluorescent lights flickered once, twice. The library seemed to exhale around her, a subtle reminder that buildings, like books, had lives of their own.

Mandy slung her backpack over her shoulder and stood. The orange carpeting—hideous as ever—squished beneath her boots. But now she noticed other things: the way sound traveled differently in this corner of the library, creating pockets of perfect silence; the subtle patterns of shadow cast by the metal shelving; the gentle vibration of the ventilation system that felt almost like a pulse.

Heading toward the exit, she passed the empty circulation desk where a forgotten mug of coffee had gone cold, leaving a perfect ring on a stack of return slips. The night security guard, Bernie, dozed in his chair near the entrance, a paperback western splayed open on his thigh.

"Another late night?" he asked without opening his eyes, startling her.

"Research waits for no one," she replied, the familiar exchange comforting in its predictability.

She pushed through the heavy glass doors into the February night. Frigid air slapped her cheeks. She wrapped her scarf around her mouth and nose and pulled the hood of her quilted parka over her head.

The campus sprawled before her, streetlights casting pools of amber on snow-dusted walkways. In the distance, the carillon tower's illuminated clock face showed 3:17 AM. She'd been in the library—both libraries—for nearly six hours.

Yet she didn't feel tired. If anything, she felt more awake than she had in years.

The walk to her efficiency apartment took her past the Red Cedar River—not the same stretch where Jack had died, but water that had flowed from that place, carrying its secrets downstream. She paused on the pedestrian bridge, resting her forearms on the gray metal guardrail, watching the water rush through this narrow stretch, past the ice-caked riverbanks.

Her apartment welcomed her with its familiar smells: old coffee, the lavender sachet her mother had tucked into her Christmas package, the faint mustiness of a building that had housed students since the 1950s. Mandy kicked off her boots, shucked her backpack, and collapsed onto the sagging green corduroy couch, not bothering with lights.

Sleep claimed her immediately, deep and dreamless.

WHEN SHE WOKE, watery morning light filtered through blinds she'd forgotten to close. The events of the night seemed impossibly distant, dreamlike. Had she really found a phantom library? Nearly unraveled reality in her desperate attempt to save her brother?

She sat up, rubbing her eyes. Her backpack lay where she'd dropped it, research materials zipped up tight. Real enough. Her finger showed no trace of the silver tool's puncture.

Something white caught her eye—a small square on the floor near the door. A library card. Not the plastic MSU ID she used, but something older, made of thick paper with an elaborate border. No patron name was printed on it, just a blank line. But in the top corner, a small red squirrel was embossed, its eyes catching the light from impossible angles.

Mandy picked it up, running her thumb over the embossed squirrel. Patron privileges, the best gift a baby academic could receive.

She placed the card carefully in her wallet, though she somehow knew she wouldn't need it to find her way back.

Mandy moved to her kitchenette, really just a shelf, a sink, and a double burner, filling the kettle for coffee. Outside her window, students in puffy coats trudged through new snow to their morning classes. Would they believe an impossible library existed alongside their ordinary world?

A cinderblock-red squirrel darted across a nearby branch, pausing to watch her through the glass with knowing eyes before disappearing into an iced-white cedar tree.

The grief remained, would always remain. But it sat differently now. Less like a stone and more like a seed.

The kettle whistled, calling her back to the present moment. Outside, the winter sun broke through clouds, making the snow-capped campus glitter.

Mandy cradled her coffee mug between cold hands and smiled. She had research to continue. A thesis to finish.

A life to live.

CURE OF THE CENTURY

THE HORROR WAS in the waiting. Watching others fall silent, one by one, eyes wide with panic as words abandoned them. Wondering when you would be next.

First Senator Michaels during a live presidential debate, her face bewildered panic, her mouth opening and shutting mid-rebuttal, nothing coming out but silence. Then other politicians around the globe. Soon, everyone who spoke.

Teachers froze mid-sentence. Lawyers found themselves unable to complete arguments. The clerk at the convenience store stomped his feet in frustration, but still couldn't tell you what shelf the axle oil was on.

Language itself was under attack.

They called it Senator's Disease—Rapid Neurological Language Deterioration too clinical, too removed from the terror of watching someone you loved get lost inside their own mind. Families stopped speaking altogether, desperate parents communicating through hastily scrawled notes while children watched in confused silence.

The wealthy fled to isolation compounds while others gathered in silent prayer circles, communicating through touch and tears. Only essential workers ventured out regularly, and even they used speech sparingly, uncertain if frequency of language use correlated with infection rates.

It didn't help.

The disease seemed like it was coming for everyone, everywhere. The world grew quieter as humanity retreated from its most defining trait.

Day ninety-seven after the first case, and still no explanation. Government and corporate research facilities worked around the clock while conspiracy theories flourished. Was it a bioweapon? A mutation in language-processing neurons? Divine punishment?

Chloe Samir had taken a rare night off from EsCorp to have Sunday dinner with her mom when her mother pointed frantically at the salt shaker, terror flooding her eyes as she realized the words she wanted were gone. Within a week, her mother couldn't form a coherent sentence. By next morning, she couldn't recognize her own name written on paper. The pattern had repeated with ruthless efficiency—language centers systematically destroyed, leaving her trapped in a wordless prison.

The call from Esther came the morning of her mother's transfer to long-term care. The repurposed hotel sat in a woodsy part of Dearborn, a short bus ride from downtown Detroit, where EsCorp was based.

"We need you here," her boss had said, the melodic quality in her synthetic voice carrying an urgency Chloe had never heard before. "We're seeing patterns in the global data. Your neural interface work might be the key." After six years as

Esther's lead researcher, Chloe knew that tone—Esther had found something.

The three-story brick and glass building in Detroit's manufacturing district had transformed in the past months. The modest facility where Chloe had spent countless hours developing testing protocols for Esther's breakthrough medications now hummed with desperate energy. Scientists from competing labs—from competing countries—had joined EsCorp's data network, drawn by Esther's unique processing methods and the synthetic human's remarkable capacity to see connections others missed.

Together, they accomplished the impossible. They confirmed which neurons were being decimated, developed a synthetic molecule to restore them, and repurposed a known-safe viral vector to get it through the blood-brain barrier and into the withered neural pathways.

They witnessed its success first in Senator Michaels herself, Volunteer Zero, who progressed from wordless frustration to halting speech in just two weeks. Within a month, the first test batches of the new molecule were being delivered to Ontario, whose healthcare networks could handle the continuous observation and reporting needed to confirm the effects. Soon after, Detroit had set up clinics and hospitals enough to run a second wave of testing. Chloe herself took part in this second wave.

While Michigan's data collection had been inconsistent at best, the monitoring systems hastily implemented during the emergency rollout, the Canadians already had a comprehensive tracking system in place.

No matter who was measuring, the results were spectacular. Nearly everyone learned to speak and understand language again, in more or less time. No one who took the treatment as a preventive contracted the disease later.

Now everyone wanted the cure, right this second. Nobody asked about side effects or long-term impacts. They saw only salvation.

EsCorp had shared its formulation freely, but growing the vector took time, and formulating the molecule was not child's play. Getting a shipment direct from EsCorp's two modest manufacturing facilities was prized more than gold.

Who could have predicted that salvation would come from a city once synonymous with American industrial collapse.

CHLOE LIKED TO BE THOROUGH. She leaned forward in her wheelchair, the scent of antiseptic from the cleaning crew's recent passthrough making her squint at the holographic display. The cleaners had left the space around her alone, but every surface in the open-plan office was shiny, stinky clean, including the fake-wood table her display hovered above.

"Samir," she said to her computer, "overlay test subjects 127 through 342." Her voice echoed in the empty lab. The rest of her team had scattered hours ago, escaping to celebrate the shipment schedule's moving up by two weeks. Through the lab windows on the second floor of EsCorp, Detroit's winter twilight had transformed the skyline into a constellation of lights, latticed by the snow that fell in thick clumps and melted against the heated glass with soft, irregular taps.

The display rippled, multi-colored neural pathways stacking over one another like translucent spider webs. These late scans looked beautiful, really. Formerly ravaged language centers now flickered with renewed activity. Mom's scan was in this group somewhere. Chloe had forced herself not to look for it.

Not that it mattered. The scans looked nearly identical. Like all the others.

The breeze from the lab's hyperventilation system slipped through the weave of her blue-and-gold cardigan sweater, raising goosebumps on her arms despite the warmth radiating from the equipment surrounding her. She rubbed her chilled legs and then tucked her hands into her sleeves.

Something didn't taste right. But it wasn't here, in the outer networks. Chloe rubbed her eyes, feeling the grit of fatigue.

"Okay, let's focus on the temporal processing region." The display zoomed in, highlighting sections on the lateral edges of hundreds of brains. Decision-making pathways. Reaction centers.

"Now overlay pre-treatment and current scans with temporal markers."

The graph stuttered.

"Slow it down, please. Way down."

At one-sixteenth speed, she could see the difference. The red pre-treatment flows didn't line up with the green post-treatment flows. Just the slightest bit off.

Chloe pulled up her keyboard. She wanted to see the real numbers, not just the pretty pictures. The raw data.

There—between impulse and action—a 48-millisecond extension in processing time.

In every single subject.

"Can't be right," she muttered, fingers flying across the tactile keyboard. The keys clicked rapidly beneath her touch, their slight resistance offering the physical feedback she preferred over voice commands for complex operations. The sound blended with the hum of the lab equipment and the distant rumble of factory machinery on the floor below.

The chair beneath her suddenly felt too hard, its armrests digging into her flesh as she gripped them. A calibration error? A glitch in the scanning equipment? A bug in the cure's nanobots that they'd somehow missed? Whatever it was, they needed to fix it.

She needed to talk to Esther.

THE CORRIDORS of EsCorp after hours always unsettled Chloe—too quiet, too clean, the motion-activated lights creating pools of sterile whiteness that followed her down the long hall toward the executive elevator. The data stick felt warm against her palm, as if the evidence of something unexpected buried within humanity's miracle cure were an underground fire about to explode.

She passed the break room where a wall-mounted screen silently displayed news footage: crowds outside a Detroit clinic, people weeping with joy as family members spoke their first sentences after weeks of silence. The scrolling ticker beneath showed distribution figures that made her stomach tighten: OVER 2.3 MILLION TREATED WORLDWIDE • CANADA REPORTS 98% RECOVERY RATE • ASIA ROLLOUT EXCEEDS PROJECTIONS.

The elevator whisked her upward, its transparent walls offering a dizzying view of Detroit spreading below. Strings of headlights traced the grid of streets, their glow diffused by the falling snow. She'd grown up watching this city transform—abandoned auto plants becoming sleek laboratories, empty towers filling with engineers and scientists. She'd also witnessed the transformation of synthetic rights—from the Detroit Autonomy Riots when she was a teen to the landmark case Nakamura v. United States that finally granted synthetics personhood status.

The scent of the elevator's cedar rails and front panels—one of the original owner's quirky touches, insisting on natural materials where possible—mixed with the faint metallic scent that permeated Motor City, especially here close to the Detroit River.

Her phone buzzed with a notification. Another trending story about the cure—this time a viral video of a former linguistics professor giving his first lecture since recovery, students giving him a standing ovation as he fluently discussed phonological theory. The comments section over-flowed with heart emojis and declarations that EsCorp deserved a Nobel Prize. One comment with thousands of likes read: "Worth any price. I'd give everything I own for this cure."

She clicked off her phone, her stomach knotting tighter. The world wasn't just eager for this cure; it was desperate for it. EsCorp had four full crews on manufacturing, working six-hour shifts around the clock. Trucks and trains rolled in to the big doors at the far side of the building, loading up and heading out at all hours.

She hadn't noticed any unusual side-effects in herself since taking the treatment. Nothing that would raise alarm bells. Just the miracle of keeping her language while others lost theirs.

But 48 milliseconds… what did it mean?

But what would a pause in distribution mean for the millions waiting? For those partially through their treatment course?

"Floor three," announced the elevator in a gentle voice, the doors sliding open silently.

The entry leading to Esther's office felt warmer than the rest of the building, the temperature already set to ease Chloe's perpetual cold sensitivity. Esther knew she was coming.

Chloe's fingertips tingled against the textured control pad of her wheelchair as she navigated toward the familiar doorway. No one was at the greeting station, it was so late.

The weighted door slid open with a soft whoosh, releasing a subtle waft of sandalwood and beeswax. Esther's office was an odd but comfortable combination of high-tech sterility and old-world craftsmanship.

The square room held angles and shadows. Moonlight sliced through tall windows on one side, highlighting the empty conversation pit, a slight depression in the floor with four arc-shaped stuffed sofas covered in plain sailcloth forming an open circle and a brass rail circling it, and then the high-polished wood boat of a desk beyond. The wood gleamed honey-gold, not a single data pad or coffee mug marring its surface.

Chloe pushed forward, taking into account the slight resistance of the plush carpet against her chair's treads. In the silence, she could hear the hum of the building's systems, the soft click of the environmental controls adjusting to her presence.

"Esther?" she called, her voice sounding smaller than intended.

She spotted her boss then, standing near the far wall just out of the moonlight's path, looking out the far window toward the city. Stiff and straight, arms crossed, the silhouette almost unnaturally still.

Chloe had watched Esther evolve over their years together, from the wooden, too-precise CEO with the flat affect of an AI assistant to the nuanced, almost-human leader she was today. Esther's skin caught the light with a fine-grained luster—a reflection of her maker's maritime passion. In his will, he had given her his company, his fancy home in Grosse Point, and his three gorgeous handmade sailboats.

Chloe rolled toward her. As she neared, their gazes caught in the window's shallow reflection, and Chloe felt her heart rate accelerate. Something about Esther's posture—the precise angle of her shoulders, the perfect stillness—told Chloe something was off.

Esther stepped fully into the light now, and, as always, Chloe couldn't help but notice how deliberately she moved. Each gesture precise, nothing wasted. Unlike the early synthetic humans with their awkward gaits and unnerving stillness, Esther had been designed to mimic humans, even down to selected micro-imperfections: the occasional blink that lasted a millisecond too long, the slight asymmetry in her smile, the way she sometimes brushed her hair from her face unnecessarily.

Her skin held the luster of enhanced dermis, laboratory-grown to mimic the slight translucence of human tissue but engineered to resist aging. Only the triangular burn that started at the back of her right hand and sprayed up her wrist disrupted the illusion of perfection. Acid, from an anti-synthetic protestor who'd gotten too close three years ago at a press conference.

The incident had occurred just weeks after the Property Reclassification Act, when synthetics were legally recognized as sentient beings rather than owned technology. That legislation had triggered violent backlash: manufacturing plants burned, synthetic shelters vandalized, and a wave of "decommissionings" that most people now acknowledged as mass murder. Esther had become a reluctant symbol of the movement when she refused to press charges against her attacker, instead inviting him to a televised dialogue that had changed more minds than any protest.

On the wall to the side of the conversation pit, a bank of screens displayed distribution centers worldwide. Live feeds from Singapore showed workers in blue uniforms loading crates onto autonomous delivery drones. In Frankfurt, a line of refrigerated rail cars waited at a dedicated platform. São Paulo's footage revealed trucks with studded tires ready to deliver to remote regions. Each screen had its own data tracker, showing thousands of doses being administered by the minute.

"Three hundred million people treated as of this morning," Esther said, her voice carrying that faint melodic quality that sometimes betrayed her synthetic origins. She looked off to the left, reading a notification only she could see. "EsCorp production says capacity at 127 percent. Additional resources required."

Chloe swallowed, suddenly unsure how to explain the problem. If it was a problem.

"So, I noticed something in the latest scans. An anomaly.

Consistent across all subjects. So far." She fumbled with the data stick, suddenly eager to let the data talk instead of her. She held the cigarette-lighter shaped stick out, toward Esther.

"The cure is extending neural processing time by exactly 48 milliseconds," she said.

Esther pivoted slightly to look at her, tilting her perfect head. Her blond bobbed hair brushed her chiseled jawline. "Perfect."

The word hung between them, heavy with meaning Chloe couldn't decipher. Her fingers tightened around the data stick, its hard end digging into her palm.

"We need to consider pausing distribution. Run some more tests."

"Why?"

What? "Esther. There's a glitch in the cure. It's changing people's brains beyond the disease repair."

"Chloe. It's not a glitch."

The world seemed to tilt slightly beneath her.

Not a glitch.

Not an error.

Outside, a sharp tone pierced the air. Another production alert. Through the windows, the loading area below hummed with activity, automated carts moving crates onto trucks and into shipping containers. Millions of doses already distributed. Millions more in production.

"You… you did this on purpose?" The words felt strange in her mouth, disbelief coating each syllable. The data stick slipped from her suddenly numb fingers.

The screens on the wall flickered. Another distribution milestone reached: Johannesburg's treatment center switching from amber to green as they completed their first thousand patients. A soft chime indicated success.

"I didn't hide anything from you specifically," Esther said, tapping the brass rail around the conversation pit as she passed it and approached the massive desk. Her fingertips brushed across its sleek wood surface in a gesture Chloe had seen hundreds of times. A quirk programmed by the boat-builder who'd created her, who'd instilled an appreciation for craftsmanship in his synthetic daughter. "I simply didn't high-light a secondary effect that would have complicated the approval process."

The statement hung in the air between them, cool and matter-of-fact. Chloe inhaled sharply, drawing in the competing scents of the office—sandalwood from the panels, beeswax from the furniture polish, Brasso, and the faint, clean smell that always surrounded Esther, something like fresh linen but with an undercurrent of warm electronics.

Esther called up a floating screen over her desk. Before she switched to a spreadsheet, Chloe read the alert at the bottom of the screen. "DISTRIBUTION OUTPACING PRODUCTION – RESOURCE ALLOCATION DECISION REQUIRED NOW."

"That's not your decision to make!" She pushed her chair forward, stopping just short of the desk.

The words sounded melodramatic even to her own ears, bouncing off the slick surfaces of the office. Through the windows, Detroit's neon-new skyline was hidden by dark lines of sleet.

"Do you really think we could pause now?" Esther asked, her tone conversational, as if discussing a minor scheduling conflict. "Three million people already treated. Global health organizations reporting miraculous recovery rates. Governments worldwide have staked their reputations on this cure." She gestured toward a news feed showing the president of India touring a distribution center, smiling for cameras. "The cure works. What would happen if we suddenly announced there might be a problem?"

Chloe's mouth went dry. The implications washed over her. Panic, distrust, chaos. People refusing to come back for the second dose. The disease going chronic. Politicians demanding investigations. EsCorp dismantled. All progress halted.

"Forty-eight milliseconds. Every single patient. That's not random, Esther. That's deliberate."

Esther smiled—one of those micro-expressions that had looked so odd to Chloe at first and now seemed totally natural —and swiped the floating screen away. She gestured toward the conversation pit.

"Let's discuss this properly," she said.

Chloe hesitated, then followed Esther down the slight ramp that spiraled alongside the brass railing. The vibration of her wheelchair changed subtly as it adjusted to the incline, a sensation so familiar she rarely noticed it anymore. Tonight, her heightened awareness made every detail feel significant— the slight warmth radiating from the floor heating beneath the carpet, the way the lighting dimmed slightly as they entered the pit, as if responding to the tension between them.

Esther settled onto one of the padded-sailcloth sofas. Her movements were fluid yet precisely economical—never wasting an inch of motion, a habit that had once seemed uncanny but now felt simply… Esther.

She swiped her hand through the air, and a data projection materialized between them. "Canada's three-month data is comprehensive. These are the crime statistics."

Chloe scanned the figures, her analytical mind automatically searching for patterns despite her overwhelm. Every category showed decreases. Violent crime, down 62 percent. Domestic abuse calls, down 78 percent. Even traffic accidents had fallen by half.

"Could be coincidence," Chloe said, though she didn't believe it. The metallic taste of adrenaline lingered on her tongue. "Correlation doesn't equal causation."

"Of course." Esther's tone was measured, patient. She lifted up the padding of the seat beside her to reveal a refrigerated cooler. She pulled out a small carton of cranberry apple juice and handed it to Chloe. Then she changed the data projection. "Which is why we have this."

The display jumped to security footage from what appeared to be a Canadian shopping mall. A man in a business suit bumped hard into a teenager with bright blue hair, sending the boy's purchases flying. The man's face contorted with anger, his hand rising—then something strange happened. A visible hesitation, a flutter of confusion across his features, and the raised hand diverted to help collect the scattered items instead. The timestamp indicated this was from a region with 87 percent of the population dosed.

"That's..." Chloe struggled to find words, the implications dizzying. She made herself open the carton and take a small sip of juice as her thoughts raced. She swallowed "That can't all be from just a 48-millisecond delay."

"It is," Esther said, leaning forward. For a moment, her perfect composure slipped, and Chloe glimpsed something like passion behind her engineered features. "Most human brains decide to perform an action about 500 milliseconds before the person performs it. But no one consciously realizes that they intend to do something until 150 milliseconds before they act."

The explanation hung in the air, scientific and precise. Through the windows, Chloe could see the sleet had thickened, muffling the city sounds. The only noise in the office was the soft hum of environmental systems and her own staccato breathing.

"So, all you actually have time to do is veto whatever act your regrettably biased subconscious had decided on." Esther continued. "This … tweak gives you a bit more time—half a eyeblink—to think. That's all. Just enough to bypass the most primitive responses."

Chloe held that idea in her mind. She compared it to her own thought processes tonight. She'd felt panic—righteous anger at potential danger—when she'd discovered the anomaly. But instead of immediately screaming "Stop!" she'd analyzed the data first. She'd considered multiple possible explanations. She'd come to Esther.

Was that this new delay at work? Or was that her "natural" delay?

A memory surfaced—college roommates marveling at her calmness during disputes, her ability to defuse tense situations with measured responses. "I wish I could stay cool like you," one had said after a particularly heated argument with her boyfriend. "I always say things I regret."

"Where are the crimes of passion now?" Esther said. "The spur-of-the-moment misdemeanors? The support calls for family abuse? Nearly gone."

She swiped to another screen—news archives showing the Synthetic Registration Riots, the public deactivations during the early Synthetic Containment era, the infamous Congressional hearing where a synthetic child had been disassembled on live stream to "demonstrate they feel no pain." Chloe remembered watching that footage in college, the hollow feeling in her stomach as the synthetic child's pleas were dismissed as "programmed responses."

"We all need this…delay?" she asked.

"No," Esther said, her voice softer now. "Remember your EEG during the job interview?"

Chloe's mouth went dry, despite the cranapple juice. Six years ago, she'd been surprised by the brain-scanning test during her interview—unusual even for a company as thorough as EsCorp. The memory suddenly replayed in vivid detail: the cool electrodes against her scalp, Esther watching the readings with that too-intense stare, the slight tilt of her head when a particular pattern emerged. Had Esther been scanning for this specific trait all along?

"You mean…" Chloe's voice faltered as her mind rewound and replayed that part of her history. "The job offer, our friendship, all the late nights working together—was it all just because my brain already worked the way you wanted everyone's to work?"

The betrayal felt physical, a hollowness spreading beneath her ribs. Six years of partnership, of shared breakthroughs and setbacks, of coffee and takeout and laughter—had it all been calculated?

Chloe had been hired for her brain, sure. But it wasn't just her knowledge, or her skills. There was something in the raw material of her thought that Esther valued.

Something Esther was now replicating in millions of unsuspecting humans.

Hundreds of millions.

Billions.

Had Esther been studying her all along, using her as a template for this cognitive enhancement?

"You've been planning this from the beginning?" The realization settled like ice in her stomach. "Since before Senator's disease even appeared?"

Esther's expression shifted subtly—not quite amusement, not quite pity. "No. But opportunity and preparation often intersect."

"So you're what—trying to fix us?" Chloe asked. "Making humans more like synthetics?"

"Making humans more like their best selves," Esther corrected. She flicked her wrist, and the display shifted to show a composite neural image—thousands of brains overlaid. "There is always variation. Some humans, like you, already have longer processing times. More deliberative cognition pathways. Less reactive impulses. I studied the brain scans of thousands before finalizing the tweak."

Chloe's hand moved unconsciously to her throat, feeling her pulse race beneath her fingertips. The carpet's texture suddenly felt abrasive against her wheels as she adjusted her position in her chair.

"But you're changing people fundamentally without even telling them."

Through the windows, delivery vehicles continued their relentless movement across the loading area, carrying the cure —and its hidden cognitive "enhancement"—to distribution centers worldwide.

The reality of what was happening crashed over her again —this wasn't a hypothetical ethical debate. This was already done. Hundreds of millions already affected.

"Would you have consented?" Esther asked, her voice nearly a whisper. "If someone had told you: 'We have a cure for Senator's disease, but it will also extend your impulse control by 48 milliseconds, making you less likely to act on your worst instincts'—would you have said no?"

Chloe's thoughts raced. Would she have refused? Would anyone? The cure meant lives saved, families restored, humanity's most precious gift preserved. What was a slight cognitive adjustment compared to that?

"But it should have been my choice," she insisted. But her conviction wavered. Her gaze dropped to her own hands, the fingers that had trembled with righteous fury now still against the controls of her chair. "I might have said yes. Others might not. That's the point."

"Sure, Chloe," Esther said, in that tone she used when explaining concepts to investors—patient but with an edge of condescension that scraped against Chloe's nerves. "Say, 'Hey, people of Earth, I'm reprogramming your brain a teensy bit, okay?' That would go over well. Especially after a synth created it."

"And now what?" Esther asked. "Shall we announce to the world that their miraculous cure has a side effect? Watch how quickly humans turn against us?" She gestured to another screen showing the latest anti-synthetic incident—a medical assistant model vandalized just blocks from EsCorp. "They're already looking for reasons to fear us."

"You went into biotech for a reason," Chloe said. Time was running out.

Esther nodded. "When Thomas was killed," she said, referencing her maker's murder by anti-synthetic extremists, "I inherited his philosophy. Humans and synthetics need to coexist. But humans..." She gestured toward the window, toward the world beyond. "Their impulses make coexistence difficult. Dangerous."

The cuff on her blouse slid up, revealing more of the triangular burn. Chloe winced at the sight—synthetic skin didn't heal like human tissue. The damaged area would remain unless surgically replaced, a permanent reminder of human volatility.

Chloe turned her attention back to the statistics still hovering in the display between them. The dramatic reductions in violence, in impulsive crimes, in rage-fueled destruction. The numbers swam before her eyes, blurring as she considered the implications from this new angle.

"Humans fear what they don't understand," Esther said. "Your species has a remarkable capacity for both compassion and cruelty. The cruelty almost always stems from impulse—from the primitive parts of your brain that evolved for survival, not coexistence."

Chloe's hands moved unconsciously to the rims of her chair, fingers tracing the familiar contours. Her relationship with technology had always been complicated—rejecting some interventions while embracing others. Her hover-equipped chair wasn't "fixing" her; it was a tool she'd chosen to navigate a world not designed for her body.

Could Esther's lie do some good? Didn't the truth always come out in the end? What would humans think of synths then? There already were enough horror stories of researchers invading people's privacy, and even harming them. But this wasn't harm.

Was it?

Esther turned to look at the bank of screens on the wall.

One showed a social media dashboard tracked since the early trial announcements. Sentiment analysis showed overwhelming positive response—97 percent favorable mentions across platforms. Video clips showed political rallies where speakers promised to "fast-track this miracle to every corner of the globe." Religious leaders called it "divine intervention through human ingenuity." Comment threads contained millions of personal stories—people begging for access, offering their life savings, describing loved ones in various stages of the disease.

How could she say no?

Chloe backed away from Esther. She took the ramp out of the conversation pit and went back to the bank of windows. Outside, new trucks and shipping containers, wet with sleet, had replaced the earlier ones. But it must be getting colder again—the sleet had turned back to heavy snow.

The thick cobalt flow of the Detroit River had disappeared behind the whiteness, but she knew it was there. Barges crawling upstream, bringing raw materials to feed EsCorp's manufacturing pipeline, and the other three manufactories, in Michigan alone.

Another notification chimed—another milestone reached. Another million doses administered. The process unstoppable now, momentum building with every passing hour.

What did this all mean? Could it even be reversed?

Would she want it to be reversed?

She certainly didn't want to put Esther in danger.

"So, it's only epigenetic," she said. The question felt crucial, hanging between them in the quiet office. "Right?"

"The change will last two generations, maybe three,"

Esther confirmed. "If it isn't useful, we'll start to see the hair-trigger humans popping out again then."

Chloe closed her eyes, her lids heavy with the weight of billions of lives. Two or three generations. Not permanent, but long enough to matter. Maybe.

She thought of her mother, who'd lost language and found it again. Of the professor giving lectures once more. Of the man in the mall whose raised hand had diverted from violence to help. Small moments of connection rather than conflict.

Then she thought of consent—the foundational principle of her work. Every clinical trial, every test subject had signed pages of disclosures. They had chosen to participate. But now, all of humanity hadn't been given that choice.

"What about transparency?" she asked, opening her eyes. "Don't we have a responsibility to tell people? After the immediate crisis has passed, at least?"

Esther's mouth turned down. "And risk a backlash against synthetics? Against you? Against everyone who helped develop this cure?"

The implications hung heavy in the air. Chloe understood the calculus Esther had made—weighing abstract principles against concrete outcomes. The cure was saving lives. The modification was reducing harm. The math was undeniable, even as the ethics remained murky.

What if the roles were reversed? If a human had modified synthetic cognition without consent? Well, didn't humans do that all the time? The double standard was uncomfortable, but so was the reality of human history—a long record of impulse overriding judgment, of fear triggering destruction.

Chloe thought of the early anti-synthetic riots, of Thomas

Corrigan's murder, of the synthetic child disassembled on live stream. The acid burn on Esther's arm. All products of that hair-trigger response the modification was designed to temper.

Two or three generations. Enough time to see if this change truly benefited humanity, without permanently altering the species.

Her reflection stared back at her from the window glass, superimposed over the snow-muffled city beyond. The face looked both familiar and strange, as if she were seeing herself from a new angle.

"And it's safe?" Chloe asked finally, the scientist in her still reaching for data points.

"Exhaustively tested," Esther said, nodding toward the fallen data stick. "Continually. No adverse neurological effects. No cognitive impairment. Just… a moment. A pause. Space to think."

"They'll blame it on the disease," Esther added, as if reading Chloe's thoughts. "We've all been exposed to it. When neurologists eventually notice the pattern shift, they'll attribute it to Senator's Disease itself or the recovery process."

She could live with that. For two generations, maybe three.

Chloe nodded slowly, feeling the heft of the decision settling into her body. Her chest released. Her mind felt strangely clear.

"Okay. So. We need to think this through."

"We?" Esther's voice held a smile, a hope. She held the data stick out to Chloe.

Chloe took it, and dropped into her technical manager mindset. "Right. We need to document everything. Research protocols, the full effects, all the data. Make it easy to read."

The thought eased her heart somewhat—creating a record

for future generations to understand what happened and why. A kind of deferred consent.

Esther studied her face, synthetic eyes scanning for uncertainty. "You're sure?"

"No." Chloe said, with a grimace of a smile. "But yes."

Outside, snow continued to fall over Detroit, trying to muffle the city beneath its hush. But the steady hum of voices would continue to rise.

THE MEMORY BAZAAR

AYA HURTLED DOWN PENNSYLVANIA AVENUE, her Doc Martens slapping against the pavement. She was cutting it close to catch the last north-bound Green Line train of the day.

The Maestra "high-performance" espresso machine at work had pooped grounds all underneath itself and onto the floor. How, Aya had no idea. But cleaning all that up took way too long.

The November wind bit at her exposed skin. At least the breeze had swept the red maple and yellow ginkgo leaves onto to the grass, leaving the wide sidewalk clear. Nobody was out; even the valet parking folks had retreated behind the Capital Grille's steamy windows.

It wasn't two blocks to the station from the giant glass-fronted building she'd left behind. Home to Johns Hopkins's Washington, DC, extension and the café where Aya did the work part of her work-study. The problem was she had to cross two wide streets that even at 11:22 at night carried traffic that did not pay attention to pedestrians. Even pedestrians wearing bright red woolen pea coats.

She let the late-left turn have its way, and then raced across 7th Street. Archives-Navy Memorial Metro station was just ahead, its gaping concrete maw of an entrance a dark triangle behind the nearly bare trees that usually hid it. Her breath came in sharp bursts of vapor. Still, she was glad for the cold, or she'd be sweating.

Two minutes. Two minutes before the last train to College Park arrived. And departed.

It could be done. She could do it.

Her black messenger bag thumped against her hip as she ran, heavy with workbooks on cryptography and intelligence analysis. The weight of her worries dragged on her shoulders along with strap of the the bag—deadlines, work hours, weekend gigs, and that looming master's capstone project she couldn't even get her arms around yet.

Project Memoria, she'd tentatively titled it: something about integrating human memory structures into cyber-intelligence. But the ideas had crystallized into something brittle and unyielding, frozen at the conceptual stage. Every time she tried to warm up to it, to make it flow, it remained stuck. Stubbornly solid. Like grief.

Just this afternoon, she'd spent hours building complex diagrams and algorithms, creating the perfect technical framework, only to stare at her beautiful, soulless model and realize it solved nothing. Pure analysis, no intuition. Data without context. She'd slammed her laptop shut in frustration.

Her Nani would have known how to thaw it.

"Analytics without heart is just counting," Nani used to say, tapping Aya's forehead, then her chest. "Both need to speak to each other." But Nani had taken her wisdom—and her forty years as a cryptanalyst—with her, and left only echoes Aya couldn't quite grasp.

But she couldn't stall now. She couldn't miss this train. No way she could afford an Uber, or a long, cold walk.

The plaza in front of the station's entrance stretched out like a concrete moat—the Navy memorial, sombre and cold. Aya made a hard right, and then another, and hit the top of the nearest of the three parallel escalators at a near-sprint. Taking the steps two at a time, she blessed the angels that there were no clueless tourists clogging the way. The first metal panel of the drop gate that would eventually close the station for the night hung overhead, a suspended guillotine waiting for midnight.

The fluorescent lights flickered overhead, casting her shadow in nervous, elongated shapes as she ran across the red tile through the short tunnel and toward the turnstiles. She fumbled with her phone, nearly dropping it as she pressed it against the turnstile's circular fare panel. She held her breath for the two seconds it took the mechanism to make the connection, relief washing through her when the green light blinked and the machine chirped its approval. The metal arms of the turnstile clattered as she pushed through.

A gust of air rushed up from the platform below, an artificial wind tunnel created by an oncoming train. It snatched at the scarf she'd used to hold back her long black hair. Aya clutched at it with one hand, feeling the wool catch against her short fingernails.

That must be her train.

"Come on, come on," she muttered, choosing the stairs over the second escalator. Her boots clattered on the concrete steps as she descended, the sound bouncing off the arched white honeycomb ceiling. The familiar underground scent enveloped her. Stale air tinged with burnt brake pads, the metallic tang of the rails, and that weird shiny dust that seemed to coat everything underground. The light had that institutional quality—too white, too harsh—that seemed to freeze everything it touched for a fragment of a second, like a stop-motion film.

She burst onto the platform, chest heaving. She'd made it. The train was still rumbling toward her.

From the wrong direction.

Her gaze immediately flew to the electronic departure board hanging from the ceiling. The northbound side—her side, the College Park side—was completely blank. No trains listed. Her stomach dropped. On the southbound board, white letters: "Branch Avenue—1 min."

Aya pulled out her phone: 11:25 PM. The College Park train had departed at 11:24.

Shit.

"No, no, no," she whispered, willing the numbers to change, to go backward. Her voice was swallowed by the cavernous space. The platform was deserted.

Her phone's lock screen glowed beneath the numbers. That photo from the last New Year they'd celebrated together, steam rising between two teacups, her Nani's bent hands gesturing mid-story. Aya had meant to change it months ago, a year. But something in her couldn't let go of that final winter together.

She swiped it away for the moment, looking for the rideshare app. At this hour, and crossing the DC border, the fare would be at least twenty-five dollars. Money already promised for next month's rent, or her mounting student loans, or, you know, food. She dropped her head back, staring at the honeycomb of noise-dampening tiles that made up the ceiling of the platform. How well could it absorb screams of frustration?

As Aya lowered her gaze, a sliver of light caught her attention. One of the glass-fronted, upright ad displays—this one holding a backlit poster extolling the virtues of a trip to Puerto Rico—looked like it had been kicked hard. But the angle was odd.

The surface of the glass was split by a jagged crack that ran diagonally from corner to corner, and someone had scrawled white chalk graffiti across the happy tourist's face: "Freedom!"

Aya stepped toward the ad. It couldn't have been a kick—that would have left damage in a circle, or a small crack. Not this lightning-long one.

She tugged her bright red wool coat tighter around her shoulders, the color a stark contrast to the institutional mud browns of the station and the frame of the ad display.

The glass was clean as a mirror. Aya studied her reflection: dark circles smudged beneath her eyes, the Hopkins-blue scarf woven through her black hair like a river through mountains, her mouth set in a tired line. Behind her reflection, the empty space where the train should be, the sign on the wall that should have been blocked by train cars.

She exhaled, and her breath fogged part of the center of the glass. But it was way too warm here to see your breath. As she watched, the crack in the mirror's surface pulsed with a faint blue light—so subtle she thought she'd imagined it.

A puzzle.

She reached out, her fingertips pressing against the cold surface where her breath had left its mark.

The glass yielded like water, caught her wrist in its undertow, and pulled her in.

The world twisted, elongated, then snapped back into focus. She was still standing, but the world had changed. Soft silence embraced her. No trains. No ventilation hum. No crackling overhead voices. Just the soft shush of scattered snowflakes drifting down.

Aya stood at the edge of a beech forest, a couple steps from a small round pond, its frozen surface glittering under the light of lotus-shaped lanterns that hung suspended in the air. The lanterns glowed a warm pinkish white, warming at least the color of the winter landscape surrounding them. Above, stars glimmered in patterns she'd never seen. No moon, but not true darkness either. The air tasted sweet, like fresh water with a hint of honey.

Aya blinked, slow. She touched her chest. Warm, alive. Heartbeat calmer than she would have expected, as fast as her thoughts were buzzing.

Okay, wow. Time to go back. This was all a bit, well, Narnia. Aya needed to get home, get some rest, get pumped for her next drone-life day. Not have a stroke, or hallucination, or whatever this was.

She turned, expecting to see the back side of the ad. But behind her was only a sheet of ice, standing upright like a Metro-ad-sized inverted doorway. Through it, she could just make out the dim outlines of the train platform, as if viewing it through frosted glass.

And on the terra cotta tile, her black messenger bag.

With her life inside.

How could she not have missed that familiar weight on her hip? Panicked, she pressed against the ice, so cold it burned her palm. And did not give at all.

For a minute, she didn't move, frozen like the door. Frozen like the pond water, even though her heart was now hammering its staccato panic.

Her phone. Had she dropped that, too?

No, it was in her pocket. She gasped in relief, and pulled it out. Pressed on Maps.

No service.

Where was she? When? Aya tried to think. To remember. Nothing like this pond near Archives station. Had she gone back in time? Sure, Dorothy.

No good panicking. She needed more data.

Each breath she took still created small clouds that lingered, but they dissolved into sparkling motes for a moment before vanishing. And her shiver was gone. The tightness in her chest loosened as she inhaled deeply, filling her lungs with winter-bright air.

Couldn't go back. Forward it was, then.

She turned away from the not-a-door and looked at the pond again.

Around the perimeter of the frozen water, a dozen wooden booths formed a perfect semicircle. Each was crafted from what looked like driftwood and polished ice, carved with intricate snowflake patterns that caught the lantern light. So they must have those little blowtorches, like the ice sculptors at National Harbor had that one time.

She strode toward the edge of the lake, each step producing not the expected squeak of fresh-packed snow but a faint musical note, as if the world itself were a massive instrument. No wind, so when she stopped, everything went still.

Slowly, the stillness was broken by a low, mellifluous humming that seemed to come from across the water. Like the lullabies Nani used to sing. The melody tugging at something deep within her memory, something from before deadlines and career paths and the grad student grind.

As she moved toward the ring of booths, her shadow stretched long and blue across the pond's surface, dancing with the reflections of the lotus lanterns overhead, swinging in the not-wind.

Despite their odd components, the booths reminded her of the ones at the Maryland State Fair. Boxes with roofs that leaned back, and three tall sides and one short, with a counter, where the seller stood.

The nearest booth glowed brighter than the others. Behind a counter of polished driftwood stood a broad-shouldered black man with salt-and-pepper locs held back in a loose tail. His navy waistcoat embroidered with swirling patterns that mimicked the falling snow; the collarless long-sleeved shirt underneath it pristine white. His eyes, when they met hers, sparkled with recognition, though Aya was certain they'd never met. Yet something in his gaze reminded her of her Nani's—that same knowing look that saw past what she said to what she needed.

"Welcome, traveler!" His voice boomed out, warm and resonant. "Just in time for the evening's last exchange."

Aya slowed more the nearer she got to the booth. The man —his counter displayed a small weathered-wood sign reading "Stan's Orbs"—smiled broadly.

"I'm sorry," she began, "I don't know where I am. I was in the Metro station and—"

"And now you're here," Stan finished with a wink. "The Last Stop. It happens." He gestured to the space around them. "The Glimmerwood Bazaar welcomes all who have a need."

But Aya's gaze was drawn to the objects that hovered above Stan's counter and behind his shoulder. Globes made of a thin mesh that held frozen lotus petals suspended in mid-air. Each petal held a tiny dot of light. The orbs pulsed gently with their own rhythm, like breathing or heartbeats. Within them, the color-bright petals swirled—gold, silver, soft blue, and hints of rose—each one forming what looked like a scene in miniature, glimpses of moments preserved in perfect clarity.

"What are they?" she asked, reaching out but stopping short of touching.

"Dream-orbs," Stan replied, his voice dropping to a conversational volume now that she stood before him. "Each contains a joyful memory—a moment of laughter, revelation, or wonder." He gestured to the glowing booths that encircled the pond. "We use them everywhere."

Aya studied the orbs. Within one, she thought she glimpsed children sledding down a snow-covered hill; in another, dancers whirled beneath a canopy of stars. In a third —her breath caught—she could swear she saw her and Nani's kitchen, sunlight streaming through the window as hands kneaded dough with practiced patience.

"Is that...?" she began, reaching toward it.

"Only you can see what's inside," Stan said. "The orbs reflect what we've lost—or what we're afraid to remember."

"They're so beautiful." Aya's analytical mind clicked into gear. These weren't just pretty glass baubles—they were memory capsules, tagged and sorted by emotional tone. Like a geotagged intelligence feed, but for feelings instead of locations. If only real-world analysts could query witness memories as easily as these merchants seemed to access their orbs...

She paused, surprised at herself. Here she was, in this impossible place, and her first instinct was to catalog, analyze, find the pattern. How her Nani would tease her, "Always trying to solve the magic trick instead of enjoying the wonder."

"I can feel both," Aya whispered to herself, almost experimentally. She let opened herself to the wonder of it all. The way the orbs pulsed with life, how they responded to emotion, the authentic connection they created. Not just data storage but preservation of feeling.

A thought struck her: What if her project's failure wasn't about missing technical elements but about forgetting the human purpose behind the technology?

She'd been so focused on the architecture that she'd forgotten the architect.

"Something amusing you?" Stan asked, raising his left eyebrow and then wiggling it.

"Just realizing something," Aya said.

Stan nodded, then fixed her with a knowing look. "Would you like one?"

Her gaze snapped to his. She wanted one. That kitchen one.

But her wallet was her messenger back, back at the station. Probably on its way to lost and found.

"I couldn't possibly afford—"

Stan laughed, the sound rolling across the ice like distant

thunder. "We don't treat with money here. Our currency is much more dear."

He reached into the hovering mesh and plucked a single lotus petal, cradling it in his broad palm. "One true story that made you laugh until you cried. That's the price of a dream-orb."

Aya blinked, surprised. "A story? That's all?"

"That's all," Stan confirmed, though the gleam in his eye suggested it might not be as simple as it sounded. "But it must be true. It must be yours. And it must have brought both laughter and tears."

She hesitated, shifting from one foot to the other. The packed snow sang softly beneath her. "And if I tell you a good story?"

"Then you earn this." Stan held up the lotus petal. It hovered two inches above his palm, glowing amber from within. "One petal to guide you onward. Where it leads…" He shrugged, his shoulders rising and falling like mountains. "Depends on what you seek."

Aya glanced back toward the ice-door through which she'd entered this strange place. She thought of the expensive Uber, the capstone project she couldn't even get started on, the weariness that had become her constant companion. What did she have to lose?

"Alright," she said, straightening her shoulders.

Stan's eyes crinkled with pleasure. He gestured to a small found-wood stool at one end of his counter. "Sit, traveler. Share your tale."

Aya's fingers traced the swirling patterns embedded in the white-padded seat. The icy material felt almost warm beneath her fingertips. The sound it made was almost like… no.

Not that story.

She pushed that thought away and focused on finding a café story. "It was my second week as a barista," she began, her voice tentative in the crystalline air. "I was working the morning shift at the campus coffee shop—still learning the rhythms, the regulars, all the complicated drink orders."

As she spoke, the lotus petal in Stan's palm began to glow brighter, casting amber light across his face. He nodded encouragingly, leaning his elbow on his driftwood counter and setting his chin on his hand.

"I was distracted that morning, planning the timeline a wedding reception I was helping with that weekend. My second job," she explained. "My mind was on table arrangements and playlist disputes when the dean of my department walked in."

The memory unfolded before her: the bustling coffee shop, squeaks and steam rising from the espresso machine, the line of harried students and sleepy professors. She could almost smell the rich mix of coffee beans and warm milk.

"He came to the counter and all he said was, 'My usual, please.' Very crisp, very certain I would know what that meant." Aya shrugged. "I had no idea who he was, let alone what he usually ordered. But I didn't want to admit it."

Stan's eyes twinkled with anticipation. Around them, the humming in the air seemed to harmonize with her words, as if the realm itself were listening to her tale.

"I was trying to catch my coworker's eye, hoping she'd bail me out. She called something over her shoulder that sounded like 'triple shot latte' as she rushed past with a tray of pastries." Aya's hands mimicked the frantic movements of that morning. "So that's what I made—a triple shot latte, extra hot, just to be sure." The orbs floating above Stan's counter pulsed in unison, like an audience holding its breath.

"The dean took one sip," Aya continued, her voice rising with the memory's momentum, "and his eyes went wide. I swear, they bulged like a cartoon character's. Then he did the most spectacular spit-take I've ever seen." She gestured broadly, illustrating the spray. "Coffee went everywhere—across the counter, the mini-display case, and me. I was spattered, standing there in shock, coffee dripping into my apron pocket."

A small laugh escaped her, echoing across the frozen pond. In the distance, the hanging lotus lanterns swayed slightly, as if stirred by her amusement. "The entire shop went silent. Everyone staring. And then the dean, still sputtering, managed to gasp: 'I'm actually a tea guy. Chai tea latte.'"

She shook her head, remembering the mortification and the absurdity colliding in that moment. "I couldn't look up. I wanted the floor to just swallow me whole."

Stan chuckled, a warm, rolling sound that matched the glow of the petal in his palm.

"But then," Aya said, her voice softening, "the dean started laughing. Not angry laughing—real, genuine laughter. He said it was the most alert he'd felt in years, and maybe he should reconsider his beverage choices." Her smile widened at the memory. "The whole shop broke into laughter. Even me, standing there dripping with coffee, laughed until my eyes watered."

She touched her cheek, recalling the strange mix of embarrassment and relief. "I thought I'd be fired for sure. Instead, the dean comes in every morning now and orders 'the Aya Special'—Chai with a wry comment on the side."

As she finished, the humming in the air crescendoed briefly but soon settled back into its gentle rhythm. Stan's smile spread across his face like sunrise.

"A fine tale," he pronounced, his voice rich with approval. The lotus petal in his palm rose slowly, spinning once before drifting across the counter toward Aya. It hovered before her, pulsing with golden light. Tentatively, she extended her hand, and the petal settled onto her palm—warm and impossibly light, like holding a sunbeam.

As it touched her skin, she noticed the dream-orbs above Stan's booth glowing brighter, pulsing in a synchronized rhythm. "What is it?" she asked.

Stan looked up at the orbs. "The Bazaar feeds on authentic emotion, you see. Stories like yours—ones that blend joy and sorrow, embarrassment and relief—they're the purest fuel. Each genuine tale strengthens the boundary between worlds, keeps this place intact." He gestured to the dream-orbs. "That's what I collect. The emotion behind the stories is preserved in the orbs, sustaining us when the long night falls."

"You like it here?" she asked him.

"Better than the alternative." Quieter, she could see that. More serene, at least. Plenty of puzzles, looked like. Stan sighed. "I do wish there was more variety in the food. I'm a bit tired of pork buns."

"And you," he pointed to the lotus petal in her palm, "have places to go. Let your petal guide you to what you seek. A fair exchange—your story's energy for guidance."

Aya stared at the petal. It weighed nothing, yet she could feel its presence—a gentle pressure, a subtle warmth against her skin.

"How?"

"Keep it close," Stan said. "And listen to what it tells you." He stepped back from his counter, offering a small bow. "The bazaar closes soon. Best be on your way."

As if responding to his words, the petal in Aya's palm rose a few inches, drifting toward the far side of the frozen pond. It paused, waiting.

Aya stood, tucking her hands into the pockets of her coat. "Thank you," she said to Stan, though she wasn't entirely sure what she was thanking him for.

Stan nodded once, smiling wide. "The stories we tell shape the paths we walk," he said. "Yours has only just begun."

With a last glance at the glowing orbs above Stan's counter, Aya turned to follow the drifting lotus petal. It guided her past the other booths—one that sold colored-crystal figurines that moved only when seen in her peripheral vision, another displaying icicle flutes that were playing themselves in haunting harmonies. She wanted to stop and explore each on. But she also wanted to be home and safely asleep sometime this night. So she let the petal's gentle tug lead her onward.

As she reached the far shore of the frozen pond, she saw a path winding between stands of silver-barked trees. Their branches, bare of leaves, were dotted with tiny ice crystals that chimed softly in the still air. The path curved gently down-ward, leading into a small hollow where a structure took shape against the starlit sky. An amphitheater. Three rows of wooden benches faced a small stage protected by a tarp roof that looked like it was made of yellow silk. The benches gleamed as if polished by countless visitors, though none were here now. On the stage, a single figure sat upon a low wooden stool holding what looked to be a small harp.

Her footsteps muffled by the softer snow, Aya approached

slowly, trying not to startle the person on the stage. The lotus petal drifted ahead, its glow intensifying as it neared the stage. The person looked up from her instrument—a pale woman with severe features softened by the silver streaks in her dark hair, which was pulled back in a loose knot. She wore a soft gray cloak over a high-necked black dress, her posture regal.

The woman's posture—back straight, hands poised with careful grace—sent an unexpected pang through Aya's chest. How many evenings had she watched similar hands, weathered but elegant, moving across piano keys in the fading light? Her Nani had played like the music was a conversation between her fingers and the universe.

The harp was gorgeous—a 24-string lever style, dark wood inlaid with mother-of-pearl. When the woman plucked a single string, the note resonated with such depth that Aya felt it in her bones, like hearing the voice of winter itself, distilled into a perfect tone.

"So you've brought a story to the bazaar," the woman said, her voice low and melodious. "Now you come seeking a way home."

The lotus petal drifted onto the stage, hovering beside the harpist's shoulder as if whispering secrets. The woman nodded once, her eyes—gray as the winter sky—fixing on Aya.

"I am Maestra Darya," she said, her fingers caressing the harp strings without pressing them. "Keeper of the return-chord."

Aya stepped closer, drawn by the authority in the woman's voice. "Return-chord?"

"The passage that will carry you back to your world," Darya said brusquely, as if that were obvious. She gestured toward the other side of the pond, where Aya had first arrived. "Those who enter must earn their exit."

A chill that had nothing to do with the wintry air ran down Aya's spine. "Stan didn't mention that part."

A smile flickered across Darya's stern features. "Stan deals in dreams and memories. I deal in passages and futures." Her fingers struck a chord, the sound rippling through the amphitheater like birdsong. Kind of like a biometric key, only here it was emotion and narrative unlocking the portal, not fingerprints or retinal scans.

Aya wondered if the same principle could work for authenticating users in a security system—voice analysis of personally meaningful phrases carrying emotional weight.

"To earn your way back, you must sing me a line you have never dared to voice."

What?

Aya played that sentence back in her memory. Her throat went dry.

"I'm not a singer."

"This isn't about talent," Darya said, the harp strings humming sympathetically beneath her fingers. "It's about truth. One line, sung from the heart—that is the price of return."

"But why singing?" Aya frowned, her mind busily working the puzzle. "Why not just speak the words?"

Darya's fingers stilled on the harp strings. "Because what is given must balance what is taken. You've received guidance —" she nodded toward where the lotus petal hovered, "—and insight from this world. To pass back requires equilibrium." Her fingers traced the edge of her instrument. "Speaking is easy. Singing requires surrender."

Aya processed this a moment. "It's a security system," she said slowly, "but based on emotional authenticity rather than verification protocols." The realization was cascading now, connections forming rapidly. "Where I live, we use passwords and biometrics—things that can be stolen or faked. But emotional truth…" She looked up at Darya, something dawning in her eyes. "That's much harder to counterfeit."

Her project was stuck because she was treating emotion as data to be analyzed, not as the key itself.

Darya smiled faintly. "You begin to understand. The strongest security doesn't reject the foreign—it discerns the authentic."

The lotus petal spun slowly in the air, its glow reflecting in Aya's eyes. She glanced back toward the bazaar, hidden now by the silver trees. Only part of Stan's booth remained visible, a distant point of light across the frozen pond.

Aya closed her eyes, searching. Music had never been her strength—she was all analytics and strategy, deadlines and details. Yet as the harp strings vibrated in the still air, suddenly she was seven again, fighting sleep while someone sang in the dark.

No.

This was too big an ask.

"What happens if I can't… if I don't have a song?" Aya asked, her voice small.

Darya's expression hardened. "Then you remain, until you find one." She struck another chord, this one darker, more urgent. "But I think you already know what you must sing. It waits in your memory, like a bird perched on a branch, ready to take flight."

Nani's voice, falling to a sweet hum as little Aya's eyes

drifted shut. It was the sweetest memory, the most private. Just them, alone, safe in the night.

"I have a line," Aya admitted, her voice barely above a whisper. "But I've never sung it. Not once. Not since she…"

Darya nodded. "Excellent."

The lotus petal drifted closer, warming Aya's face. She opened her mouth.

No sound came.

Her vocal cords simply refused to vibrate that way.

Darya frowned, tilted her head. Waiting.

Aya swallowed. Took a shaky breath. She'd just been talking; singing wasn't so different.

This wasn't real, this place. It wouldn't hurt her at all to sing a little bit. But her throat was burning, and behind her eyes, burning.

She closed her eyes, felt them filling up. Took another rattle of a breath.

Then:

"Hush now, dreamer, the stars guard your sleep."

The words emerged rough with disuse, carrying the weight of every night she'd kept them silenced since Nani's passing. She pushed through. Her voice cracked on 'dreamer,' steadied on 'stars,' and by 'sleep' had found something she'd forgotten she'd lost. The permission to remember without drowning in grief.

As the last syllable left Aya's lips, Darya's fingers swept across the harp strings, releasing a chord that Aya felt rather than heard—a vibration that passed through her body like light through glass. The return-chord vibrated through her, and Aya felt something crack. Not like the mirror, but like spring's first breach in river ice, the moment when what was frozen begins to move again.

Motes of light swirled around her ankles, then rose to encircle her waist, her shoulders, her head. The lotus petal darted forward, touching her forehead with a flash of warmth before joining the swirling lights.

Suddenly, the petal's light seemed to split into thousands of tiny points, each carrying a fragment of her sung line. The notes of her voice, made visible, spiraled upward like stars returning to the sky.

"Wait," Aya called, reaching toward Darya. "What is this place? Why was I brought here?"

The Maestra's sharp features softened. "You weren't brought, Aya Montojo. You found your way." She struck one final note on the harp, a sound like distant bells. "And now you've found your way back."

The swirling lights intensified, becoming a vortex that lifted Aya off her feet. Then everything shuddered again, stretched, and snapped back into focus.

One of the glass-fronted, upright ad displays—this one holding a backlit poster extolling the virtues of a trip to Puerto Rico—looked like it had been kicked hard. But the angle was odd.

Aya stumbled, her boots catching on the brown tiles of the Metro platform. The glass-fronted ad display stood before her, ordinary and unremarkable, its surface reflecting only the fluorescent lights of the station. No crack visible.

She gasped, feeling as if she'd been underwater and had just broken the surface. The station sounds rushed back—the distant rumble of trains, the hum of ventilation, the muffled burble of the overhead announcements. She turned, half-expecting to see the frozen pond and the glowing booths of the Glimmer Bazaar, but there was only the Metro platform, nearly empty at this hour.

Nearly empty?

She grabbed her messenger back and pulled out her phone. The screen read 11:22 PM.

Aya blinked, certain she must be reading it wrong. She'd missed the 11:23 train—that's how this all started. But as she stared at her phone, the minutes changed to 23. Two minutes before she'd entered the mirror world.

A low rumble vibrated through the platform, a screech in the air growing louder and louder. The northbound Green Line train to College Park pulled into the station, right on schedule. The doors slid open with a pneumatic hiss, revealing the brightly lit interior.

She hesitated, glancing back at the standing ad display. Had it all been a dream? A hallucination born of stress and exhaustion?

Then she felt it—a weight in her coat pocket, a gentle warmth against her hip. Slipping her hand into the pocket, her fingers closed around something impossibly soft and light. The lotus petal. It glowed faintly through the fabric of her coat, a secret sun she carried with her. As she withdrew her hand, the petal seemed to dissolve, its essence seeping into the lining of her coat, leaving behind only a lingering warmth and the faintest scent of honey and snow.

Aya stepped forward, boarding the train just as the doors began to close. The car—one of the old ones with the hard orange-pad seats—was half-full. Sleepy people with their eyes closed or half-lidded looking down at their phones. She found an empty seat and sank into it, her mind reeling.

As the train pulled away from the platform, she thought she heard, beneath the grinding of wheels on rails, the distant, smoky notes of a 24-stringed harp. She closed her eyes, letting the melody carry her homeward. The familiar lurching of the car lulled her into a state between waking and dreaming, where images from the Glimmerwood Bazaar flickered behind her eyelids: Stan's knowing smile, the hovering dream-orbs containing fragments of joy, Maestra Darya's fingers dancing across harp strings.

Wait.

Aya's eyes snapped open. The dream-orbs. Each containing a memory, a moment preserved like amber. Stan had called them "dream-orbs," but they were really memory containers—data, stored in crystalline form, accessible to anyone who knew how to read them.

Aya sat up straighter, her heart quickening. And the bazaar itself was a kind of… network. A repository of emotional intelligence. Her fingers flew to her pocket where the lotus petal had been, finding only the lingering warmth of its dissolution.

But the idea it had sparked remained, growing brighter with each passing second. What if her capstone project could explore the intersection of memory and data? A system for encoding emotional intelligence alongside raw information—making cybersecurity more intuitive, more responsive to human patterns?

She fumbled in her tote bag for her laptop, nearly dropping it in her excitement. She opened a new document and began typing frantically, her fingers barely keeping pace with her thoughts: "MASCI Capstone Proposal: Project MEMORIA—The Memory Bazaar Framework for Emotional Intelligence Integration in Cybersecurity Systems"

The words flowed as if dictated by some invisible force. All the questions that had stalled her for weeks now had potential answers. The dream-orbs were the perfect metaphor for emotion-tagged memory storage. Stan's storytelling exchange demonstrated narrative prompting. Darya's return-chord showed how authentic emotional expression could serve as high-security verification.

What if protective systems could recognize when someone needed help before they even asked? Like Stan seeing her exhaustion and offering exactly what would restore her—not interrogating or blocking, but opening pathways.

She sketched it out frantically—not firewalls but bridges, not barriers but beacons. A system that learned your patterns not to profile you, but to notice when you were struggling. Like a grandmother who knows you're sick before you do, who appears with soup and soft songs.

The dream-orbs hadn't trapped memories—they'd preserved joy to share when someone needed light. What if digital guardians could work the same way? Recognizing distress patterns in hospital systems and alerting the right caregiver. Sensing when a student was overwhelmed and suggesting resources, connections, breathing room.

Her advisor would want threat models. But Aya saw care models instead—systems that protected by understanding, that secured by supporting. Not watching for reasons to harm or hold, but watching for reasons to help.

The train rattled through a tunnel, lights flickering overhead. Aya barely noticed. Her fingers banged on the keyboard, drawing connections between memory storage, pattern recognition, and emotional response metrics. She was vaguely aware of other passengers glancing curiously at her feverish typing, but she couldn't stop. The idea had seized her completely.

By the time the train announced "Final stop: College Park," Aya had sketched out an entire framework. She stared at the screen in wonder. This wasn't just a capstone project—it was potentially revolutionary. A way to make digital security systems more human, more adaptive, more alive. Like a frozen memory realm that thawed just enough to let in a lost soul.

The technical details could come later. Right now, she had something more important—a vision of machines that could learn wonder. As she gathered her things to exit the train, Aya felt something brush against her cheek—a phantom touch, cool as a snowflake. For a moment, she thought she caught the scent of lotus blossoms and winter air.

She stepped onto the open-air platform, the late-night chill greeting her. But the cold no longer felt like an enemy to be endured. Her phone buzzed with its midnight notifications, starting with a reminder about the afternoon meeting with her capstone advisor. For the first time in weeks, Aya smiled at the alert instead of feeling dread.

She had something to share now.

She began the walk toward her apartment, the brisk wind stealing the fog from her breath as soon as it left her body. In her mind, the outline continued to develop, algorithms and emotional patterns weaving together in a never-before-heard melody.

Tomorrow would still be tough—another barista shift, classes, the weekend wedding rigamarole. But now she moved toward them with purpose, with a vision of technology that could guard dreams as carefully as that frozen realm had guarded memories. Security that felt like being held, not being watched. Like Nani's kitchen—a place of both rules and nurturing.

Aya looked up at the winter stars, bright and clear above the neighborhood of sleeping little brick houses. For the first time since the funeral, she let herself fully remember: evenings spent measuring spices by instinct rather than recipe, stories told without books, the way her Nani had taught her that precision and intuition weren't opposites but partners in a dance.

"Hush now, dreamer," she whispered to herself, the words no longer locked behind her lips. "The stars guard your sleep."

THE RESCUE

ELLIE TOOK perverse pleasure in sloshing through the reflection of the early moon—and maybe a star or two?—on yet another flooded lawn. She followed its course, stomping through standing water all the way out to mom's lakeside cottage, alone on a tiny jut into the bay. She'd left her rental car at the village post office / town hall / emergency center; they'd told her she'd have to hoof it the rest of the way. And they shook their heads.

Sometimes, she just could not believe her mother. The woman could resolve satellite orbits in her head and browbeat university punks into politeness, yet refused to listen to an eminently reasonable flood evacuation order. "We're made of mostly water, anyway," she'd said cryptically when Ellie called last night. That, and a stern text from the township's sheriff's office, had driven her up here. Maybe mom was fading. Was this some backhanded call for help?

Well, to judge from how fast she was out the door and across the lawn, she'd lost none of her dash. "I told you not to come."

But she reached for Ellie's messenger bag, managing to stroke the side of her face in the process. "Oh, Ellie. Take those wet boots off. I'll make you something warm." Mom's shoes were still dry, like her lawn. The house must be on a slope, though it didn't look it. She turned toward the house, her jet-and-salt hair neatly tied and smooth like always when she expected company.

"Wait." Ellie stopped. The water in her boots stopped a second behind. "Was this a ploy to get me to come visit?"

"Of course not." Mom didn't stop, didn't turn around, didn't meet her eye. "Any packages in town for me?"

Ellie trailed in her wake. "They said you had to sign for it yourself." She had the package in her bag, a slick little box heavy for its size, but subterfuge was fair in this fight.

"Fine. We'll paddleboard over tomorrow."

"Mom, you'll be in the hotel tomorrow. I booked us a room."

The striped ponytail swung hard around. Eleanor Castile Sr. crossed her arms, shoulder bag and all, and scowled, a look that had set undergrads to quaking for twenty-odd years. "We're completely safe here."

But Ellie could give it right back, hands fisted, one shoulder back, hip out. And mouth shut. They'd once been so close they could have had this standoff using just the muscles of their eyebrows. Now it took their whole bodies.

Her mother broke first, turning back to the cottage and stepping onto the porch. "I swear, I never knew you to be such a Cassandra. Besides, we're past the worst of it. I saw it on the weather."

Ellie caught up and tugged her heel on the edge of the faux-concrete porch, slipping off a boot. The sock was a loss, its separated threads reforming as a gray glob just past her toe. At least the afternoon was balmy, for upstate New York in May.

"Lake levels are rising. I sent you the graphs. Sunny and clear, sure, but that doesn't mean no danger. It doesn't even have to flood a lot; if the ground gets waterlogged enough, the whole house could float away." She saw a shovel leaning near the door. "And your new roses, too."

Her mother just shrugged, a move that she must know drove Ellie around the bend. "House floats. It started as a boat, remember?"

Ellie tried to take a calming breath, but ended up snorting. Still, she got an idea. She jammed her chapped foot back into the boot and grabbed the shovel. She took a few steps into the odd oval of a yard, hedged by rugosa roses—don't call them pansies—and jammed the shovel into the earth.

"My lawn!"

"It's sod, mom. See? We can flip it back after." She shoved into the sand underneath and flipped it into a pile next to the sod toupee. The shovel seemed to want to fling its load even farther. "Look. The water is right here. I don't even have to dig that far."

Except the hole was dry.

Ellie frowned. They weren't on that high an incline. She hacked another shovelful, trying to reach knee-depth.

"Enough!" Mom appeared at her shoulder, grabbing for the handle.

"No. The emergency guys said it was bad; I walked through water all the way out here. It must be here."

Her mother groaned. "Okay, fine. How's this? You find

water here tomorrow, I go with you. If not, you'll all just leave me be."

Ellie scowled at the hole. It couldn't change the laws of geography. It would fill up. Was that a little bit of water darkening the shadow at the bottom? "Fine."

THE COTTAGE/BOAT looked the same as she'd last seen it. Cupboards and shelves comprised the interior walls, while the long outer walls held rows of seaworthy windows. What ever had possessed her mother to buy a Scandinavian house-boat and have it installed on dry land? There were plenty of prefabs in the world. But the Ikea-familiar blond wood, the near-subliminal scent of roses, and the bright, soft pillows on the sofas reminded her of home, even here.

The familiarity of making their favorite supper—macaroni and cheese with spinach and Tabasco—smoothed everyone's feathers. Between putting the casserole in the oven and getting it to the table, they'd started talking to each other again. Safe things, like Ellie's job—"Going great"—and Mom's new workout routine. "I'm up to fifteen pushups now."

Ellie raised her glass of Rueda. "Five better than me." She had to admit, it was a cute cottage for a boat, surprisingly spacious, the closets especially clever. Her mother had moved here almost the second Ellie's foot stepped out the door to grad school.

They lingered at the dining-room table. A phone buzzed once, Mom's. She peeked at the message, her face cascading through cheer, puzzlement, panic, resolution. She put the phone back in her pocket. "Did you see Sheriff Rich in town? She said to say hi."

"Stop matchmaking. She just said we should get our butts into town, didn't she?" Ellie looked away, to not see whatever expressions her mother was going to cascade through now. She got up, and they moved to the plush pair of sofas, more like loveseats, one on each. The windows framed the bay and above, the handful of stars that could compete with a near-full moon. "How's the new telescope?" It stood ready for action at the other bank of windows, near the lakeside door.

"Excellent birthday gift, thank you. Just what I wanted."

"It was the only thing on your wish list."

"It's perfect. It is, but I prefer the sounds of the universe, not the sights."

"You do? You hardly talk about it." Mom had worked for NASA only for a few years before taking a professorship, getting married, having a child, getting divorced. But she did still have the classic Apollo spice shakers, a golden thrift-shop find, and the weird paperweights with gears suspended in plastic, one for every mission she'd been a part of. And the excellent star maps.

"It's better, now that more data is public. I can make my own charts, and sound them out. They roar, like symphonies."

"You mean like that grinding electronica music you like?" Teen Ellie had thought herself the only girl in the world who'd had to tell her mother, Turn. It. Down.

Mom laughed that deep way Ellie remembered from when she was so small she could snuggle in with an ear to her mother's chest. She pushed herself upright and got the bottle from the table to refill their glasses. The sky was so big here.

"So you didn't come up here to the edge of the country for better sky?"

"Why would you think that?"

Ellie let the question linger, trying to savor the aftertaste of the Rueda. "Kinda weird to retire the moment your kid enters your own university, but whatever. It was like you fell off a cliff." Ellie waved toward the telescope. "Or shot yourself into orbit, or something."

Her mother startled, and then eased back, her finger tracing the edge of her glass. It whispered in alto.

"It felt like you left me for no reason." Ellie clenched her toes, snuggled in thick wool mom-socks, to keep her hands from telling on her. "A chance to see your beloved stars could be a reason."

"Let the record show, you left home first, law-school girl." Mom stared deep into the glass, and then shook herself a little. "You were grown, ready to fly on your own. Besides, now we text."

Ellie didn't dignify that with an answer. Texting was for making appointments, not conversation.

Mom tucked her heels under her butt. "I don't know. Call it a midlife crisis. You do know how proud I am of you."

Wait. Ellie fought the gravity of the sofa cushions to sit up straight, suspicious. "What?"

"No. I mean, I know I don't say it enough, and you wave it away when I do. But I think the world of you. The universe. I'm so glad you didn't give up on your dream."

"I had to take the bar exam three times."

"But you stuck with it. And now look at you, changing the world, saving people's lives with your words. You never gave up."

"Yeah." Ellie swirled around a sense of pride on her tongue, blending with a new suspicion. "Did you? Give up on a dream?"

"Me?" Mom laughed that tinny laugh, the one that came out during parent-teacher conferences and faculty get-togethers. "Oh, no. I went hard for my dreams."

Now Ellie was wide awake. "Mom, is something wrong? Are you sick?"

"No, no. Nothing like that." She sighed so deeply Ellie thought she might deflate. "It's only. I wish we could talk more, about what I do." She stopped, and set the glass on the side table as if it had bit her. "What I did. Whatever."

"Why can't we?"

Mom frowned at the glass, and then picked it up again. She sighed back into the sofa cushion. "Well, I guess it all started when I got fired from NASA."

"Fired?" Ellie cast her mind back. "Not because you were pregnant?"

"I mucked up an outgoing transmission, sort of. It was on your father's watch, so that was that."

The familiar sizzle of fury toward her gametes-only parent reignited in Ellie's chest. Of course he would make sure not to lose his job, no matter what happened to anyone else. "He wanted you out because he was jealous." She crossed her arms, splashing wine on her shoulder and not caring.

Mom waved her hand, and that horrid laugh came out again. "Whoa. We must be tipsier than I thought. Time for bed. We can talk more tomorrow."

They used to talk all night, tipsy or not. But that was then, and now Ellie allowed herself to be steered to the spare room. To get to the bunk, she had to sidle through the stacks of boxes with their neat hand-written labels: soft food, cans, spices, misc. She'd never seen the room so stuffed. Mom must have overprovisioned for winter this year.

ELLIE WOKE to the plink-plonk of rain hitting the ground, drowning out the ebbing tide. Just what they needed, more water. She went to the window to pull it closed and keep the rain out. The light streaked purple red, burning into dawn.

It was not raining.

She pulled her sweater on, squeezed her way out of the room, and headed out to check the hole. Where she found her mother, in fluffy bathrobe and Marvin slippers, hosing the lawn, with particular focus on the hole. "What are you doing?"

"Making you right? It should be wet. It all should be wet." Mom bit her lower lip, like a trapped teenager.

"You're trying to trick me?" Ellie slammed her hands onto her hips, full-on Stern Parent mode.

Her mother's shoulders slumped, the spray of water from the nozzle arcing to a trickle. "I didn't know what else to do."

"You want me to leave so bad?" Wait, wasn't that what Ellie wanted, too?

"No! I want you to stay. I want me to stay." Mom raised her hands, squeezing the nozzle again, spraying water every-where. "Why can't everyone leave us be?" She saw the water flying about and let go of the nozzle, dropping it into the still-not-that-soggy hole. It ricocheted back so fast the trickle of remaining water slapped Ellie across the chest.

She jumped back, hand over heart. What was down there?

Not the septic tank; that was lashed under the house. The back-up batteries were over by the kitchen.

"Mom?" The word whisper-squeaked out of her. "What is that? It's not buried treasure."

Her mother covered her face with her hands. The rose scent of her hand lotion was stronger in the morning. She pulled her hands through her hair, mixing the colors. "It is. So to speak." She dropped her hands, and it all spilled out in one breath. "Here's the thing, right? It started when I got fired from NASA. Well, caused it, really."

"You stole something from NASA?" Ellie rolled back on her heels and slipped, her hands and then her rump meeting the sodden earth. "Where were you hiding it before?"

"It wasn't here before. Just a minute, let me finish. You know, I told you about that extra transmission?"

"You mucked it up." Ellie still couldn't believe her mother never swore.

"No, it sent out fine. But I had embedded a code in it. Some specs, that redirected it, so if anyone responded only I would get the message. I would get it first."

"You private-messaged the universe?" That didn't sound anything like her mother. Or did it? Was this the before-Ellie Mom? Ellie had never seriously considered a pre-Ellie Mom. "So ... somebody rang back?" She stared at the hole as if a snake would jump out of it.

Mom waved toward the hole. "Somebody stopped by."

Ellie blinked to get her vision straight again. She grabbed her mother's arm. "No way. You met an E.T.?"

Her mother smirked. Her mother never smirked. "You're sitting on them. Their ship."

She also never lied. Klaxons blared in Ellie's head. She

scrambled to her feet, pulling her mother with her. To the porch, onto the cedar bench. One of Mom's feet was bare. They weren't going back for the slipper. "Are you okay?" she whispered. "How many are there? Can they hear us now? Are you being held hostage?"

"Of course not. There's just the one. They are older than me, but still a kid, you know, to their people. It was kind of a joy ride, like a treasure hunt, to follow the cryptic signal." Her mother was so steady, so matter-of-fact; Ellie was finding it hard not to believe.

But still. "You talk with ... them?"

Mom smiled as if she'd solved a tricky equation. "Sure, sweetie. We text."

"You ... text."

"They like to use a lot of emojis. Turns out, folks who sign up for long-term solo space assignments are kind of loners."

"Recluses. In space." Ellie gulped a breath, deep, and let it out slow. She leaned against the wall. It seemed solid enough. Did she believe her mother? Mom certainly believed. "You met an E.T. and buried its ship in your yard."

"Their ship. Well, not really theirs. It's a long-hauler, like a space semi. I think it belongs to a relative." Her mother propped up a leg on the bench, a move Ellie called camp counselor pose, ready to dispense some wisdom. She cut it off on Mom's in-breath.

"How long has this been going on?"

Mom opened her hand, as if reading an invisible phone. "I got the first message the night after you moved out, and I drove right up here. They'd already managed to hide the ship under the bay, and thought they were safe enough. Not really, of course. We figured out how to use text short-range, and made sure it was encrypted, and I volunteered to be the beard. I had to jam sailors' sonar and details like that." She talked about it like hacking was a normal thing all mothers did.

Maybe it was. What did Ellie know of mothers?

"It was my fault they were even here." Mom shrugged. "They needed my help to find materials to fix the broken part."

"They blew a tire?"

"Less sarcasm, please. It's part of the propulsion. They got too close to our outer atmosphere and tried to back out—and pop. Everything else works fine: the growers and atmosphere and batteries, all that. They just can't get out of the gravity well. They needed someone on the inside, so to speak. To place the orders, pick up the deliveries. That sort of thing."

"So, yeah. You're just being neighborly. Wait." Ellie sat up straight. She turned to her mother, trying to read those so-round eyes framed by the frizz of untamed morning hair. She lifted a hand, reaching for her mother's. "That was eight years ago. Why are you still here?"

Mom took her hand, squeezing it. "No, Ellie, they're not holding me here against my will. It's just that nothing here works as a fix. Their atmosphere acts as a solvent to earth-made things. So they're waiting for a part to be delivered from home. It's on its way."

"Home. And where is that?"

Her mother's mouth set. "Classified."

"Does NASA know?"

"Okay, not classified. More like, secret."

"Oh, Mom." Ellie scanned the lawn, the clay piled up, that stupid hole. How could they possibly keep this a secret? Was the hole moving closer? She got up, pulling her mother to join her. She pulled them both through the doorway and into the sun-warmed living room. "When is this package due?" She could just picture a flying saucer dropping by, parachuting in some giant shiny propulsion axle or whatever.

"That's the trouble. I can't leave. It's any day now." Mom squinted at the room's ceiling as if she could see into the universe. "Well, any time this month. We got a window."

"Like the cable guy." It was too much. Ellie started counting the books on the shelf. Two blue, three red, one black, one silver, one blue, four maroon. Her free hand pumped up and down with her counting, her calming ritual. Mom squeezed gently, until Ellie looked back at her.

"It's to be a drop shipment, maybe a guided parachute? But very small, and untraceable. I took a photo of a shipping label that they were to mimic in case it went astray."

It must be the package in her bag. Ellie looked up—as if she could see it past the ceiling—and tried to get her mind around all this. What if it were her, stranded? What would it be like to have to sit in your own juices for a decade? Always breathing recycled air. She breathed out. Then again, maybe traveling the vast distances between worlds, waiting for the next adventure, wasn't so different from sitting in a house in a town, marooned in a life she didn't intend. "I bet they really want to go home now."

Mom stroked her hand, like when Ellie had one of her panics when she was small. "I'm sorry I didn't tell you. I couldn't. I promised."

Ellie turned her hand palm up. She twined her fingers with her mother's. "You just. You left."

"I could never lie to you—"

"Sure, Mom." Ellie pulled her hand back, but her mother didn't let go.

"—But I couldn't tell you the truth, either. Better just to be apart. Thank heavens, you were grown, ready to fly on your own."

At that age, Mom had been at NASA, learning to soar and trying to talk to the heavens. And then she stopped, all of it.

"Not to mention I talk in my sleep. Like you, sweetie."

Ellie started to laugh at the idea of spilling secrets to random roommates, but stopped short. That's why Mom was still alone, for eight long years. Why she always called Ellie's visits "weekends," implying that they should be short. Not letting go, but holding back. And maybe this alien, this person, did need her more. Mothers go where they're needed most.

"Well," she drew the word out, exploring the taste of this new understanding. "It could have been worse. They could have shown up in the middle of our state championship season."

"That's my girl. Always the bright side." Mom patted Ellie's shoulder, just as she always had, if at a new angle now that Ellie was the taller of the two. "How about I make us some breakfast."

"And maybe show me some of those texts?"

———

HER MOTHER MANAGED to adequately field Ellie's growing list of questions over coffee. And her visitor, named "Marble" in the phone's contact list, did seem to favor animal-based emojis.

"They never come out? And you never peeked? Not even a webcam?"

Her mother scoffed, flicking toast crumbs onto her plate. "You have to respect people's privacy, Ellie. It's part of being neighborly, meeting folks on their terms."

She hadn't remembered the sheriff until her own phone buzzed. "Bad news. The deputy is coming to the closest cross street to pick you up before noon."

Mom groaned. "They won't give up, will they?"

"No, but I think I already have what you're looking for. Er, what Marble is looking for. The sheriff gave me a little box addressed to you; said she found it on the side of the road and thought it fell out of the UPS truck."

Ellie ran upstairs to get the box, and her mother took a photo of the label. "That's it, Marble says. Perfect!" Mom actually clapped her hands together, not the least bit cynically. It was hard to doubt the truth of a visitor from another planet who could quickly text back with blinking congratulations emojis. Then Mom's face fell. "But how do we manage it when we have to go?"

When we have to go. The pieces clicked into place. Extra provisions. A house that used to be a boat, so it could be picked up and taken anywhere. A mother who'd missed out on the chance for adventure half a lifetime ago. A daughter so proud of her independence but somehow never quite ready to let go entirely.

"Mom, look." Ellie took her mother's hand in hers and held it. "When I was coming here, I was so mad. Afraid, too, of losing you. We seemed to be floating away from each other, all this time."

Her mother held so still. She didn't speak. Was she breathing?

Ellie broke first. "I wasn't going to let you go, not ever. But I see what you're doing here. I see you."

Mom leaned back, her face blanching. "What do you mean?"

Ellie held tighter. "You're leaving with Marble, aren't you?"

"Oh, honey. I didn't realize how much you needed me to stay." With her free hand, she cupped Ellie's cheek.

She leaned into the touch, savoring the moment, and then leaned away. "That's the thing. I don't need, only want. And it's your life. What do you want?"

"Oh, Ellie." Her name on her mother's tongue held the universe.

"It's fine. No, I'm fine. I won't tell anyone, at least for as long as I can keep it in." No one would believe her anyway. "We'll do something. We'll slosh into town and pile into my rental car, and then I'll drop you as close as I can on my way out."

Blood returned to Mom's face, washing it into a rosy dawn. "Really. You mean it? It's fine, really?

"Well, it's not forever." Ellie looked at the ground. "Right?"

"Fourteen months, only. Staying in-system, to get the kinks out of the new parts. They have a whole compartment ready for me. It'll hold the house and enough air and earth water for two years at least. And I can make my own recordings!" Her eyes shone with excitement and calculation. "Think of all the data."

Ellie reached for all of her mother, smooshing her into a hug. "Good. Only, I expect you to text on the regular. Like you do with Marble."

ELLIE TOOK the telescope up to her apartment's roof just before sunset. The rain had cleared, the clouds scuttling out to the bay. Alone on the roof, she pivoted the scope to look to the northwest, toward Mom's house. They'd be leaving tonight. July Fourth, when everyone's eyes would be turned toward town, toward the fireworks.

The house/boat had gone missing earlier in the month. The local paper reported that it must have lost its moorings during the spring floods. Tonight, there would be a minor interruption in the tide, hardly noticeable, and a shadow, running dark, heading up, up, up.

The sky slid into black. She couldn't wait to see the stars.

PRECIOUS CARGO

YOU KNEW you shouldn't have let her fly alone. Sure, it sounded like a good idea: an unaccompanied minor. Who would suspect? And she couldn't be prosecuted—much—if she did get caught.

But then she vanished.

When Flight 22 disappeared from the radar just as it started its descent to fogged-in Chicago O'Hare, the panic slipped in, freezing the flow of your blood. You'd been following the flight on the FAA's tracker site, sitting too long in front of the old laptop at the work corner of the dining room table, so you weren't as surprised as you could have been by the call with the area code for Illinois. "Is she okay?" was the first thing out of your mouth.

"Ma'am, this is Officer Blah." Your mind had nothing to spare to catch the name. "There has been an incident with the plane that was carrying your daughter."

You had to sit down. You were already sitting down. You had to drop to the floor, stretch out, lie still on the colorful checkerboard carpet where Lina had taken her first steps. "What happened?"

"Could you come to Chicago?"

Your breath stopped. To Chicago? Why not the moon? You couldn't really afford to send Lina to Switzerland. But you had been desperate. And now this. You forced air into your lungs. "But she's all right?" Your voice so edged with hysteria, your husband looked up from his crossword, his face alert for danger.

"Ma'am." The voice softened. "We don't know that she's been hurt."

"Where is she, then?" You swallowed the panic down, into the roiling cauldron of your gut.

"We aren't exactly sure, yet. We'd like to bring you all in. All the families. Work out our response together."

That didn't make any sense, but before you could say that he continued. "We'll pick you up at TVC. There's another family in Dearborn—we'll get them at Detroit. That's where our plane is. Then we'll come up for you. Can you be ready in two hours?"

Of course you could. But it hadn't done any good.

TEN YEARS PASS. You tried to make it work. You lost the farmhouse when the last of the bees died. You lost your beautiful orchards, those cranky Granny Smith apples, the sour cherries and the sweet. It was all you could do to pull two more seasons of grains out of the detritus. You lost Mac a year later, off to "find himself" somewhere out in Arizona. No, you actually lost Mac when you lost Lina.

Lina was her daddy's girl, and who could ever patch that hole?

And Kara, such a bossy older sister, such a protector, she never could let go. She was still living with you, didn't even go away to the fancy college despite the scholarship. Got a working degree, then a job as a short-haul pilot, flying routes all over the Midwest. She's never spotted the plane, never found Lina. But she never stops looking, never closes that door, never lops off the broken branch so the tree can survive.

You watch Kara diminish, bit by bit. Her friends fall away. She stops going out after work. She goes days without speaking. You feel yourself withdrawing too, circling in. One morning, you see in Kara's gaze that faraway look that scared you so much when you saw it in Mac's eyes.

At last, you decide: We can't go on like this.

You can work corporate farms anywhere, even as far as California or Maine. Kara can take loads from here to there anywhere. You call old friends who used to own farms too.

Then the ads start popping up: online, pinned to the message board at the bodega. *Workers needed. One-way trip, room and board paid. Adventure!*

You broach it with Kara over Sunday lunch. She's been thinking about it, too. She says, this planet holds nothing for us. She says, why *not* the moon?

FARMING on the moon is critical infrastructure. People have never been more respectful to you than now. You're not just some worker bee here. Kara helps out for a year, and then the council discovers she's a pilot and she trains to do short hops between bases, too. You find it peaceful in the open warehouse-sized greenhouses, with their stacked plantings creating splashes of bright colors and familiar smells under the grow lights. You're surprised to also find comfort in the closer spaces of the settlement, seeing all the families thriving on what you've grown. Among you all, you'll figure out how to pull even more life out of the humus-fed local soil yet.

You can never go back, now. It's been twenty years since you left Earth's gravity, and your spine couldn't take it. It's been such a relief—such a release from the pain of a stooped back and slipping disks. Like the children here, this is your forever home. And Kara has friends—and maybe, at last, a special friend? She's being coy about it, but her eyes are bright.

You're busy when the call comes. It beeps in your earbuds, and you wave it away with a briefly free hand. Your people know to text, and besides, all these plants aren't going to pollinate themselves. You go one by one down the long rows, and up the many ladders on the walls of berries, acting like a monstrously large replacement for the long-extinct bees, carrying life from stamen to stigma, over and over. The scent of the green wheat below overwhelms the plants in front of you. You flick another wave of beeping off, and another.

Your ward chief is waiting for you as you step off the ladder. "You need to take the call."

"Kara?" The panic roars out of nowhere. It floods your bones, numbing your fingers. Not again. Not after all this time. Not her, too.

"Kara is fine. It's down planet. We should do this in a comms room, with better signal. I'll be there with you." You remember this woman's other job is counseling.

You don't remember washing your hands, walking down

the many corridors, through the many airlocks, to the private cocoon that is the secure comms station. No one uses this one anymore now that the station in the new government module has gone online.

"It's better if you stand," the counselor says, swiping what must be dirt from the side of your face. "This will be waist-up." You're not sure why they need to spend the bandwidth when voice is fine, and then you're distracted as someone in a blue-gray uniform is projected like a half-statue, a bust, in front of you. The set of their face carries professionalism, and concern, and something else.

"There's been a development in the missing-airliner case," they say.

Your body freezes, all the blood rushing through your thoughts. That seed you'd buried so deep, that tiny sprout of hope, explodes across your mind. What has it been feeding on, all these years? You're swaying. The counselor takes your hand.

"Lina?" You push the word out through the vines.

The official doesn't stop talking; there's always that delay in the relay. "The liner appeared, right where it went missing, on extended approach to ORD. It had to divert immediately, of course, and now it is at TVC—Traverse City."

You wait, and they continue: "Right, yes. Your daughter, Angelina, is safe and sound, here at the airport. But I under-stand you don't live near here anymore."

Is this a joke? "You know you're calling the moon, right?"

They look to the side then back at you. They adjust the collar of their perfectly proportioned suit. "That's a first. We're just going down the list." They touch their ear. "Yes. We're ready to transfer the call now."

You're about to topple. You need to sit down, suck up a lot of oxygen. The counselor shifts closer, moves her hand to your lower back. Holding you upright. You stiffen your knees. The image shimmers, blinks out. Another form blinks in.

It's her, round and brown and beautiful. So much younger than you remember. You realize you've been aging her up in your memories, keeping her just three years behind Kara. When she got mad at you, Kara would accuse you of trying to erase Lina, because you'd tucked all the photos of her away. Now, you realize it was to keep her alive, and growing.

Lina's face is a shade pale; tired, but so healthy! So squeezable. She was too big for squeezes now; she'd told you just last year. Thirty years ago.

The counselor squeezes your hand. You blink back to now.

"Mom! You look so old. The airport is completely different —I mean, the wood frame is still here but everything inside is weird. They have beanbag chairs here that talk to you, and give you a massage at the same time. Mine's named Sandy. Sandy says my T-shirt is a collector's item now, after we mend the little rip." Guilt flashes across her face, quickly masked by bravado. You haven't read her in so long.

"Lina. You're such a beautiful sight."

She's already off on something else. "Yeah, mom. Sandy knows everything. Can I keep it? The gray-shirts—I mean, the officials—are so worried we'll infect them, maybe they'd be glad if I took my talking beanbag with me."

You hold up your hands, like always. "Slow down, scout. One thing at a time."

"You'll have to bring the truck. It's kind of bulky. You still have the truck, right? Maybe if I look really, really sick, they'll give it to me, just to get rid of me."

She hasn't outgrown that manipulative streak. She hasn't outgrown anything, you realize. An iceberg forms in your belly. How can you raise her right when you're all the way out here on the moon? Here is your missing child, your stolen child, all alone on a wounded planet.

You change the subject. "What have they told you? The gray-shirts."

Lina groans. "Can you believe? We discovered time travel! But it only goes the wrong way, I guess. They told us about a dozen other planes did the same thing, all over the world, before they decided that no one else should fly through this weird kind of fog. Well, duh. We're the third plane back, and they *still* haven't figured it out. You heard about it when they got back, right?"

You'd stopped opening the messages, the ones from the wife of the actress, each a new blade to the ribcage. How could you have known? "Lina, love. When are they going to let you go?"

"Not sure. We're in 'decontamination' now, which is hilarious because they're more of a danger to us than we are to them, right? Evolution and all. Everybody's making calls like this, trying to find their families. I'm the only minor traveling alone, so I get first pick of the snacks. But," her face changes, "I want to come home. When can you come pick me up?"

How do you tell her? You search your mind for an answer, for something that might work.

She knows you're stalling. Her face—her perfect, cantankerous face—scrunches up. "I know. We can't afford it." She looks out, away from you.

You reach for her, but your hand glides through empty air. She turns, and reaches for you. Her face mirrors your own side-frown. You see her recognize the grimace at the same moment you do, and then the tears. Fast but quiet because we can cry all we want but the work still needs to get done.

So you suck it up, and tell her. "It's a real trip, scout. I'm on the moon."

You have not surprised her so since she was a toddler. Her whole face opens, delighted. "Seriously? How did *you* get to the moon? Is Dad there, too?"

You let that one slide. "They put me in charge of the produce part of the greenhouses. Turns out, the moon needs people who aren't fancy scientists, too."

"Wow." You watch her chew on that for a bit, and see the moment her thoughts turn dark. The iceberg chill shivers down your spine. "You left me?" The tears start up again. Your little stoic, crying? Then you remember: in her world, the poor baby has been flying for the better part of two days. She's overtired.

You want to push her hair out of her face, and wipe the crust out of the corners of her eyes. Did she even remember to wash her face today? Her sloppy, boisterous, precious little girl. "Do they have showers there? You should get in line."

She sniffs the tears back, rolls her eyes, sinks on one hip, and says your name in two syllables: "Mah-um." A flash of joy dives into your heart, even as you remember how that move used to feel like a spike to the gut. You need to touch her, to smell the peaches from her favorite shampoo, to brush that tangled hair. Put food into her, as she tells her stories in that hop-thought way no one can follow.

"Kara is here with me. She's a pilot."

"No fair! That's what I wanted to be."

You just want her. "You always did want to fly." You hear the forbidden wistfulness seeping into your voice.

"Ugh. I want to leave home, yeah, but not leave the family. I need adventure, not a dusty farm in a dusty town."

"It's pretty dusty here, sweetie."

Lina doesn't even flinch at the endearment. She's not listening to you. "Huh. I guess you got what you wanted. Remember? You said these next years were going to be so hard. You wished I could skip them, live my life in the next upswing." She looks away from you. She looks so lost. "So, is it time yet?"

That's it. You're going back. You'll find the money; you'll get a frame to support your back. "Stay there. I'm coming to get you."

Her face glooms before you even finish the sentence. Her shoulders drop, her chin sinking toward the stripes of her Hello Kitty T-shirt. "I wanted to be the hero," she says, voice in vibrato. "But I'm too late." She hugs tight to her carry-on bag, which must hurt her, with its boxy shape and sharp edges. Why doesn't she have a softer bag?

Then you remember.

"Omigod, Lina! You got the bees?"

"Duh. That's why I went, remember?" Lina's teen whine rankles, but hope overrides it. "Too late now."

"No. Not too late. Hold on." You turn to the counselor, whose face carefully controls her compassion. "The reason we sent Lina on the plane to Switzerland was to pick up bees. We'd waited for all the local ones, the ones with the blight, to die, and we were going to rebuild our hives."

"Bees?" The counselor says. "Like in the old days?" The woman is in her thirties. Lina should be forty-three.

"Yes. So, if we could get them here, then I wouldn't need every family to help me pollinate twice a year."

"Really?" Lina's voice cuts in. "I have the only good bees in the world?"

SHE LOOKS OFF-SCREEN, and then holds her bag tighter, almost stepping out of the frame. Her image wavers. You reach out. You'll never learn. You'll never give up again.

"Lina! Stay here! Listen."

She shakes her head, shades of Kara, but hits the good-video mark again. Her image firms up. "They must be listening to us. These big gray-shirts are coming my way. You can't have them!" she shouts off-screen.

"Listen!" You shout to catch her attention. "Say these words: *precious cargo*. I'm carrying precious cargo." That was the phrase you'd have to stamp on the boxes of the best cherries you shipped, to that upscale reseller. Those packages never got lost.

The counselor touches your shoulder. "I have to go make some calls. Don't worry about the bees. Or Lina. We'll get her sorted."

"Yes, it's precious, precious cargo." Lina is talking fast and off-screen now. "And only I know how to take care of it! I want to go to a good school, and learn how to be a moon-pilot. And I want to go work on the moon. And I want ... I want some bubble tea. Can we get some on the way to the Ag center? I'm going to the Ag center. I'm not letting these queens out of my sight until they're safe. You grown folk already messed this up once."

She looks back, at you. "Mom, I gotta go, okay?"

AT THE LANDING pad embarkation zone, you're rigid with more terror and excitement than one middle-aged body can stand. Kara had said she couldn't watch the landing, and waits at home. This morning she was wearing a perfume you haven't smelled in years, green-apple-candy sweet. Lina's. She must have kept it all this time.

You have to see. You had jumped through the hoops to gain access to the control center room that has the real window, so you can follow the shuttle almost all the way. The landing pad is on the other side of the crater wall, but the wall of camera views will show touchdown.

The shuttle does not disappear just before landing. The dust rises over the ridge; the usual amount of dust caused by a normal landing. It will take some time for the passengers go through decontam procedures, so you can walk to the embarkation tunnel. Good thing; your heart is throbbing so, you're not sure you even could run.

The tunnel is nicer than back when you arrived, brighter and cleaner and more welcoming. The passengers shuffle slowly, carefully, trying to stay on the ground until they get their moon-legs. The oddly ozone smell of the purifiers they've just walked through reaches you before they do. Their voices huff and murmur, as if they're afraid their words, too, could float away. You can't see Lina—these people are all too tall and bulky. They should have let her off first. You take a little hop to see to the back.

You recognize her hair first—no one else's as shiny and

silken and still so long. The shape of her walk thrums a chord in your heart. Your soul unspools, reaching out to her. She will need to put up with a hug.

She sees you and lets out a whoop. This startles her fellow travelers so much they turn and step aside, and there she is, in new black slacks and boots but still the homemade sweater you sent her off in, all those years ago. She swings her arms, and you know she's about to do her little joy-jump.

As she starts, you cross the distance in one low leap. She launches, too hard. Her arms propeller as she tries to stop her inevitable crash into the ceiling. You catch her at the shoulders, push her to safety, into your arms.

CASTING SEEDS

WHEN ADDIE PASSED by Valley Gallery's big window and looked inside, she smiled to herself. A day after the new exhibit opened, and nobody was in the spare white room. Not great for the poor painter whose work hadn't sold too well last night, but perfect for her.

She adjusted her chunky purple sweater against the March breeze. One of those false spring days in suburban Maryland that fool the crocuses into blooming but might still freeze them solid next week. The warmth felt good though, sunlight catching on her short hair that looked brown most of the time, but in direct light revealed the silver threads that had multiplied since Claude's passing.

The mocha latte in her hand was still warm, fragrant steam carrying chocolate and espresso notes that mingled with the crisp air. Food wasn't allowed in the gallery, of course, but if she kept the cup low, tucked slightly behind her large droopy hobo bag, who would notice? Especially with no one inside to enforce the rule.

Addie pushed the door open with her elbow. A soft bell chimed to announce her entrance. Nobody appeared.

The gallery smelled of fresh paint and the faint, distinctive scent of the screen press frames from the workshop area in the back. The polished concrete floor reflected the recessed lighting, creating pools of warm illumination between displays. As the heavy door swung shut behind her, the outside world receded. It was past one now—after the lunch rush but before the school kids would pile in for their afternoon classes. A perfect pocket of stillness.

She went straight to the back wall, to the painting that had caught her eye last night. "Autumn in Nantucket, 34," according to the small placard beside it. The cool white walls made the painting's warm autumn colors seem to glow from within. She could almost feel the temperature change of that depicted afternoon—the last warmth of sun against the first chill of fall. The artist might want to spend a little more creativity on titles, Addie thought, but the work itself held plenty.

The image reminded her of Andrew Wyeth—a foreground of what looked like wheat or tall grass sweeping up a hill to a small, squared-off house in the right-corner quadrant. But it was technique that had kept drawing her attention, especially the sky. At first glance, it appeared still, the palest blue. But when you stepped closer, you could see the swirls of deeper blues and whites blended with that weird edging technique she wanted to study. And the way the edging made the grasses seem to be moving.

Her fingertips tingled, eager to try capturing those edges with her charcoal pencils. Could she do it? The graphite wouldn't convey the colors, of course, but maybe she could capture that particular texture, that feeling of movement.

The way the landscape stretched toward the horizon reminded her of the travel blogs she'd been browsing lately—nomads in converted vans waking up to different vistas each morning. She'd bookmarked several listings, telling herself it was just idle curiosity, though the browser tab had remained open on her tablet for weeks now.

She pulled out one of the gray metal folding chairs stacked against the back wall and set it in front of the painting. The chair legs scraped against the polished concrete floor, the sound echoing in the empty space. Addie winced, though there was no one to disturb. Probably whoever was in the back had taken one look at her from the security camera in the corner and gone back to whatever they were doing.

Settling into the uncomfortable seat, she placed her coffee on the floor beside her—still out of sight, she hoped—and opened her hobo bag. Her sketchpad and pencil case were easy to find. She'd carried the art supplies for only a few months now, but already they felt right.

This was her third serial obsession, as she'd come to call these post-Claude pursuits. First had been the guitar—three hours of practice daily until her fingertips calloused, only to discover she couldn't bear playing the same songs over and over. Then came gardening, with elaborate plans for her postage-stamp backyard, until the neighborhood wildlife declared war on her seedlings. Even the elaborate pipes-and-netting guard she'd built couldn't deter the determined squirrels and the deer. She had retreated from that battlefield, defeated.

But this—this drawing thing—seemed to be sticking. There

was something about the way each sketch just emerged, how her hands could translate what her eyes saw in ways that surprised her. She could sketch that tulip-shaped vase on her bookshelf dozens of times, and each attempt revealed something new.

Today, something about this particular painting called to her. Not just its technique, but a certain warmth, a feeling it evoked that she couldn't quite name. Maybe it was the landscape, so unlike the suburban streets of Hyattsville but somehow familiar in its solitude.

"Let's see if I can figure you out," she whispered to the painting, her breath creating a small cloud in the gallery's climate-controlled air. She opened her sketchpad to a clean page, selected a medium-soft charcoal pencil, and began.

The first few attempts felt clumsy. Addie's pencil skittered across the paper, leaving harsh lines where she wanted softness. She'd always been methodical—a data analyst didn't succeed with sloppy work—but capturing art required a different kind of precision. She tried again, this time letting her wrist relax, the charcoal barely grazing the paper.

Better, but still not right.

She took a sip of her mocha, now cooling to room temperature. The chocolate taste had intensified as it cooled, turning slightly bitter. Like memories, she thought. Sweeter when fresh, more complex with time.

The artist from the opening flickered through her mind as she tried a third approach to those edges. A matronly figure enhanced by flowing scarves and skirt, with silver white hair pulled into a low, loose bun. Voice rich as dark chocolate, explaining her process to an admirer. Something about layering, about patience.

Patience. Addie knew about all that. Three years caring for Claude as cancer slowly dismantled him. The specialists with their technical terms, the hospice nurse with her gentle euphemisms about "the journey." All that time to say good-bye, and still, when it happened, she wasn't ready.

Her pencil paused above the paper. The painting seemed to shimmer slightly, or maybe it was just her eyes watering. She blinked hard and refocused.

Looking closer at the swaying grasses, she realized the technique might require a softer touch. Not pressing down but building up. Thin, overlapping layers. She flipped to a fresh page and started again, using the side of her charcoal rather than the point, letting it slide across the paper in gentle sweeps.

The field began to emerge under her fingers. Not perfect, but closer. She felt a small thrill, the same satisfaction she'd gotten when her vegetables first sprouted last year, before the local fauna declared war on her efforts.

Time vanished as she worked. The gallery remained empty, the only sounds her breathing and the occasional soft scratch of charcoal on paper. Gradually, she stopped looking up at the painting every few seconds. The image had imprinted itself in her mind—she could see those swirls with her eyes closed now.

As her hands sustained the rhythm of the work, Addie's mind drifted to the live-model sessions she'd been attending every other Wednesday night. Sandy, Kim's mom who ran the gallery, had encouraged her to join after seeing Addie's early sketches. "You've got an eye," Sandy had said. "But you need to practice capturing the living form."

Those nights had become something Addie really looked

forward to. The studio would fill with all kinds of people—art students with their earnest concentration, middle-aged hobbyists looking for creative outlets, twenty- and thirty-somethings with multiple agendas.

There was always that initial frisson of excitement when the model took their position—the collective intake of breath, the reverent quiet that settled over the room. Addie loved watching the human body transform into art before her eyes—not just in her own sketches, but in the very act of the model holding a difficult pose, turning flesh and bone into lines and curves, shadows and light.

She'd noticed how the younger artists often spent as much time eyeing each other as they did the model. The tentative smiles, the lingering glances as they compared sketches, the deliberate positioning near someone who had caught their interest. A dance as old as humanity itself.

Addie loved watching it all unfold—the flirting, the possibilities, the quiet yearnings—without feeling any need to participate. These beautiful young people with their hopes and insecurities laid bare in ways they could not yet see. The divorced man in his thirties who always chose the easel furthest from others but glanced around hopefully when he thought no one was looking. The young woman with the purple-streaked hair who created brilliant, bold sketches but spoke about them in whispers.

She saw them all, loved them all, and felt utterly content. No one paid much attention to her, a woman from an earlier century. Such freedom—to see without being seen, to appreciate without expectation. It had become one of her greatest joys.

In the gallery, Addie had slipped into what she called her

art trance, that meditative state where her hands seemed to know what to do without conscious direction. Peaceful, floating. But today there was something more—an odd sensation of connection, as if her pencil strokes were somehow linked to something larger than herself.

For a moment, she felt as if she weren't just copying a painting but participating in it somehow. The feeling passed so quickly she might have imagined it, but it left her oddly exhilarated.

A faint metallic scent from the charcoal mingled with the gallery's eau de turpentine. Smelled like prep for screen printing. Addie's round wooden pencil felt warm where her fingers gripped it, smooth and familiar. Outside, clouds passed over the sun, changing the light that slanted through the high windows. The gallery's careful lighting adjusted automatically, maintaining consistent illumination on the artwork even as the natural light shifted. Addie barely noticed. Her world had contracted to the size of her sketchpad, to the movements of her hands creating something from nothing. Re-creating.

The wheat field took shape first, then the small house, and finally that intricate sky. Not an exact copy—she wasn't trying for that—but her own interpretation, her exploration of how those edges worked. When she finally looked up to check a detail in the upper left corner, where the blue deepened almost to black, she blinked in confusion.

The shock of the front door banging open shattered her concentration. Voices, young and eager, spilled into the gallery, bouncing off the high ceiling and ricocheting between the white walls. School must be out.

The kids were arriving for their print workshop in the back room. The scents of playground dust, cafeteria lunch, and the indefinable energy of youth washed through the previously serene space.

Almost four o'clock. She'd been sitting here for nearly three hours.

Addie looked down at her drawing—not a fine-detailed examination like she had been doing, focusing on one small bit of it, but the whole image. It was almost done. The swirls in the sky were too dark, but she might be able to buff them out lighter. She looked up at the painting, setting her mind to focus on the luminescence of it, to see if she could get the balance better.

The painting was blank.

Addie's breath caught in her throat. Her pencil clattered to the floor as a wave of vertigo crashed over her, the room suddenly tilting sideways. She gripped the edge of her chair to steady herself. The children's voices seemed to come from inside a tunnel.

She blinked hard—once, twice, a third time—each time expecting the familiar landscape to reappear.

The canvas remained stubbornly, impossibly empty.

Not happening. Her mouth went dry, the metallic taste of fear coating her tongue.

Someone must have moved the painting while she was absorbed in her work. But that was just as impossible—she would have noticed.

Wouldn't she?

She glanced frantically around the gallery. The last of the children skipped past, the dawdlers, chattering, oblivious. None of them even looked at her.

She stood slowly, shaking off the pins and needles, and took a hesitant step toward the canvas, hand outstretched. The frame was solid beneath her trembling fingertips, the canvas smooth, gessoed, but blank. Pristinely, unnaturally blank, as if the painting had never existed. Yet her sketchbook held its echo, captured in charcoal strokes.

Sweat broke out across her forehead and down her back, making her shiver. Was she having a stroke? Hallucinating? Having a senior moment? Nothing could account for the emptiness in front of her, nor the certainty that moments ago, this frame had held a world.

Feeling guilty, furtive, Addie quickly closed her sketchpad and tucked it into her giant bag. She gathered her pencils with trembling fingers, dropping one and having to bend awkwardly to retrieve it from under the chair.

She must be hallucinating. She must need protein, or something. When had she last eaten? She couldn't remember.

Standing up, she grabbed her empty coffee cup and moved quickly toward the exit, keeping her eyes averted from the blank canvas. Outside, the bright late afternoon sun slapped her. She squinted and hurried down the sidewalk, away from the gallery. But the questions—the bewilderment—followed like a shadow.

The coffee shop where she'd bought her mocha earlier was crowded now, a line snaking out the door. Addie kept walking. She needed to clear her head, not stand in a noisy queue. At the corner market, she grabbed a protein shake instead, something she could drink while walking. While getting away from the gallery as quickly as possible.

The cool plastic bottle felt reassuring in her hand, something solid and real. As she walked up the hill, away from Main Street, she twisted off the cap with a satisfying crack and took a long swallow. Vanilla, sweet and thick.

Walking briskly now, she followed the familiar route home. The protein was already helping, steadying her blood sugar, grounding her in physical sensation. The whole thing had been a trick of the light, or fatigue, or low blood sugar. There were plenty of logical explanations that didn't involve paintings vanishing into thin air.

The neighborhood around her looked perfectly normal. Mrs. Patel, the mayor's wife, was watering her front garden, the spray creating tiny rainbows in the afternoon light. Two houses up, someone had finally fixed that sagging gutter. The brick rowhouses with their varied front porches lined the street like sentinels. Unassuming, solid, sturdy. So different from the pristine gallery space she'd just left.

Hyattsville had changed over the decades, arts districts sprouting up alongside the old hardware stores and family restaurants, but its bones remained the same. Ordinary life continued. Nothing extraordinary happened.

But as Addie's heartbeat slowed and her breathing steadied, the unsettling knowledge remained. She'd been drawing that painting for hours. She couldn't have imagined it.

College Avenue sloped gently upward as she approached her block. The row of short post-war brick houses came into view, her own standing seventh from the corner. Almost identical to its neighbors at first glance, but Claude had installed those blue shutters twenty years ago that made it distinctly theirs. She still thought of it as "theirs," even now.

She'd started to wonder if it wasn't time for a change. The house felt too big for just one person. Rooms she barely entered anymore were starting to gather dust.

The concrete walkway leading to her front steps was cracked in places, with tufts of persistent weeds pushing through. She'd been meaning to hire someone to fix it but hadn't gotten around to it. A flash of purple caught her eye— three small crocuses had bloomed along the edge of her lawn, delicate and brave.

Addie suddenly didn't want to go inside. The house would be empty and still, giving her too much space to replay the gallery incident in her mind. Instead, she sat down on the second step up to her porch, feet on the sidewalk, and placed her bag beside her. She sipped the last dregs of her protein shake and put the cap back on before dropping it into her bag

From here, partially hidden by the large azalea bush Claude had planted, she could observe the street without being obvious about it. The late afternoon air carried the scent of someone's fireplace. Pattersons, probably, always quick to light a fire at the first hint of evening chill. Underneath that woody smoke she caught the earthy scent of warming soil, of spring slowly awakening.

A car drove past, music thumping. The Warren girls next door were arguing about something, their voices carrying through an open window. Warm enough for windows up. Normal sounds, normal life.

Addie took a deep breath, and then reached into her bag and pulled out her sketchbook. Her hands trembled slightly as she opened it and flipped to her new sketch. Still there, thankfully. The charcoal image looked back at her, the field, the house, the swirling sky. But something was different. The drawing seemed to pulse, as if the charcoal lines were breathing.

She touched the paper gingerly. It felt normal—slightly textured, cool against her fingertips. But there was an energy to it she couldn't explain, as if the drawing might lift off the page at any moment.

"You have something of mine."

Addie jerked her head up, heart hammering. A woman stood on the sidewalk in front of her. The artist from the gallery, unmistakable now in the clear daylight. Up close, she had more presence, more solidity than Addie remembered, but somehow still carried that ethereal quality, as if she might dissolve into the air at any moment.

Today she wore a long, flowing dress the color of autumn leaves, her white hair indeed pulled back in a simple knot. Her face was lined but ageless somehow, her eyes a startling blue against her dark skin.

"I—I'm sorry?" Addie twisted her wrist, flipping the sketchpad shut.

The woman smiled, no anger in her expression. "May I?" she asked, gesturing to the step where Addie sat.

Stunned, Addie nodded and shifted slightly to make room. The woman settled beside her, not touching but close enough that Addie could smell her perfume. Something herbal and ancient, like dried lavender and sage.

"I watched you in the gallery," the woman said, her voice that same rich chocolate alto Addie remembered. "You have a gift."

"I don't understand," Addie said, clutching her sketchbook against her chest. "The painting—it disappeared."

The woman nodded, as if this were perfectly normal. "You took it," she said simply.

"Took it? I was just drawing, I didn't—"

"Not physically." The woman's lips curved upward. "The essence of it. The part that matters."

A chill trickled down Addie's spine. This conversation was unreal. Yet the woman beside her was undeniably real—her warmth, her breath visible in the cooling air.

"Who are you?" Addie asked at last.

"My name is Arda. Arda Samorand." She turned those piercing blue eyes on Addie. "I'm a traveler. A seeder."

"Seeder? Of what?"

"Peace," Arda said. "I seed it wherever I go. In small ways, subtle nudges. It's been my calling for quite some time."

"Quite some time," Addie repeated faintly.

"Longer than you might think." There was a hint of amusement in Arda's voice. "It's been fun. But the work, it's so incremental. I always feel as if I'm losing ground. But then something will happen, and I catch a second wind."

Addie's mind raced to make sense of this. "What kinds of things?"

"Here, it was your mayor," Arda said, gazing down the street as if seeing beyond it. "He changed his mind about those 'delinquent kids,' as he called them. Added a skateboard park and rec center to the budget this year."

Addie blinked in surprise. It was true—Mayor Carlson had done a complete about-face last month on the youth recreation issue. It had been the talk of their neighborhood meeting.

"You're saying you… influenced him? Through your painting?"

Arda shrugged one elegant shoulder. "The painting held a seed. He received it. Not everyone does."

The logical part of Addie's mind rebelled. Patent nonsense, magic paintings, seeding peace, mysterious travelers. Yet something deeper nodded in recognition.

"But I'm tired," Arda continued, her voice softer now. "I've been trying to let go."

Addie looked down at her sketchbook, understanding slowly dawning. "Is that why the painting… came to me?"

Arda laughed, the sound like distant wind chimes. "No, that was all you. I've never seen anyone do it without using oils before. Nice technique."

Despite everything, Addie felt a flush of pride. "So what does this mean? You want your… seed back?"

"I want to offer you a job," Arda said.

An oriole landed on the azalea, only an arm's length away from Addie. Its vibrant plumage startling against the dark green leaves. A migratory bird, here one season and gone the next, never settling in one place for long. Constantly moving, always following its purpose.

"A job," Addie repeated. The absurdity of it all suddenly struck her, and she laughed, a short, startled sound. The evening was settling in now, the sky taking on a lavender hue. "What kind of job involves magical paintings and invisible… peace seeds?"

"The kind that matters," Arda said, calm, unperturbed by Addie's skepticism. "You create art that carries intention, that shifts the small moments that lead to bigger ones."

The woman was serious.

"Lonely work," Addie observed, studying the other woman's face.

"It can be," Arda admitted. "But you're already comfortable with solitude, aren't you? I watched you at the gallery. You enjoy your own company."

It was true. Since Claude died, Addie had grown accustomed to the rhythm of life alone. She'd even come to appreciate it—the freedom to follow her impulses, to eat breakfast for dinner if she felt like it, to spread her art supplies across the dining table for days.

"You make it sound like I'm qualified just because I'm alone," Addie said, a hint of defensiveness creeping into her voice.

"No," Arda said. "You're qualified because you can see beyond yourself. Most people can't. They're too wrapped up in their own needs, their own narratives."

The Warren girls' voices had quieted next door. The streetlights flickered on, casting long shadows across Addie's lawn. She should go inside soon, start thinking about dinner.

Dinner. As if.

"But shouldn't you find someone younger?" she said. "One who could do this… seeding for longer?"

Arda's smile was just off center. "Like one of those kids during live-model night? Or at the teen print shop?" She chuckled. "Younger people don't know what you and I do. They haven't learned. Most of them can't even see past themselves."

"That's not just a problem of the young," Addie pointed out.

"You said it."

Arda touched her chest. "You'll be like me. You won't get older, or weaker. You will get wiser, if my experience is anything to go by."

"Say yes, and your joints won't stiffen. Your mind won't falter. Your heart will beat just as it does today, for as long as you choose this path."

Addie's breath caught. "Immortality?"

"We prefer to call it 'suspension,'" Arda said. "The work sustains us, but we can let it go. In our own time."

Addie couldn't help but stare, searching Arda's face for signs of deception or madness. But those eyes held only calm certainty and something else—a depth that hinted at decades, perhaps centuries of a life well lived.

The cool evening air raised goosebumps on Addie's arms. She pulled her sweater tighter, considering the impossibility of what was being offered. No aging. No sickness. A purpose larger than herself.

"Especially here in the States," Arda continued, "being an invisible woman is quite useful. People underestimate us, overlook us. We can work undetected."

Addie thought of all the times she'd been ignored in stores, spoken over in meetings, treated as if she were part of the background. It wasn't always a joy.

She looked down at her hands. The first fine lines that had appeared around her knuckles years ago now deepened, the skin thinner, blue veins more prominent. Hands that had held Claude's through his illness, that had learned guitar chords and planted seeds and now held charcoal with growing confidence.

"Stay just as I am now," she said slowly, testing the words. "No more loss of muscle tone or bone density." No fear of becoming frail or dependent. She looked up at Arda. "But no chance to grow old with friends either."

"You trade one kind of companionship for another," Arda said. "There's a small network of us, maybe two dozen. We find each other, from time to time. Brief convergences on the road. It's different, but not without its own kind of intimacy."

Addie thought about her friends scattered across the country, most connections maintained through screens now anyway. She thought about her neighbors, kind but involved in their own family dramas. And she thought about how she'd felt in the gallery today, that moment of connection to something larger than herself.

"How many people do you give this offer to?" she asked, her voice steadier than she expected.

"It's been a while," Arda said. "I thought I was tired back during the Sixties, but the person I found wasn't interested." She looked directly at Addie. "You are rare."

Addie did not feel at all rare. Yet something stirred inside her—the same feeling she'd had in the gallery when the painting seemed to breathe with her.

"What if I'd taken up knitting instead of sketching?" she wondered aloud.

"Could you knit a seed?" Arda asked, tilting her head. "Like, something people could wear and be reminded?" The artist frowned thoughtfully. "Maybe. Try it."

The possibility expanded in Addie's mind. Not just paintings, but all kinds of art carrying these seeds of peace. The guitar she'd abandoned, the garden she'd surrendered—perhaps those weren't failures but stepping stones, preparing her for this moment.

She glanced back at her house, solid and familiar. Yet in the gathering dusk, it looked different somehow. Less solid.

"I've been thinking about selling anyway," Addie said, surprised by her own words. And then not surprised. "This place is too big for just me."

Arda nodded, saying nothing, giving her space to follow her own thoughts.

"No kids," Addie continued. "Friends scattered, mostly

online now. And I've been feeling… restless." She looked at her sixty-three-year-old hands, then back at Arda. "How does it work? Practically, I mean."

"You'll have means," Arda said. "The art sells. People are drawn to it, even when they don't understand why. And the network. We help each other when needed."

"And I just, what? Go where I feel I should be?"

"You'll know," Arda said. "The need calls to you. Sometimes it's a whisper, sometimes a shout."

As if reacting to a shout, the oriole flushed out of the azalea. It zoomed across the street and landed on a branch of Annie Bell's oak tree, and quickly moved on. Always moving, place to place. Carrying seeds.

The evening had settled fully now, the sky deepening to indigo. Addie's neighbors were turning on lights, settling in for dinner, television, ordinary routines.

She thought about the mayor's decision, the skateboard park that would give kids a place to belong instead of being labeled as troublemakers. One small change that would ripple outward in ways no one could predict. One seed, planted and growing.

She could do that. Not just here, but everywhere she went. She wanted to.

"Yes," Addie said, the word emerging with surprising certainty. "Yes."

Arda's smile bloomed, transforming her face. "I knew from the moment you caught the edges," she said, reaching out to clasp Addie's hand. Her touch was warm, solid, anchoring.

"What happens now?" Addie asked, suddenly light-headed. What had she just agreed to?

"Now, you keep the drawing," Arda said. "It's your first seed. And tomorrow, we begin."

"Tomorrow," Addie repeated. So soon. Yet it felt right.

And terrifying. Could she really leave all this?

She looked over her shoulder, at the house. Claude's house, their house. Now it was a vessel of memory rather than a home. The blue shutters he'd installed with such pride, the worn threshold they'd crossed together countless times, the kitchen window where she'd stood watching for his car in the driveway. For three years, she'd been haunting these rooms like a ghost, clinging to what was.

She could release it all.

Her practical side asserted itself. The house could be sold, possessions donated. Her life pared down to what truly mattered. The thought was scary and thrilling in equal measure.

Arda squeezed her hand once more before letting go and standing up. "Rest tonight. Dream of where you might go first."

As the artist walked away, her figure seemed to blend with the gathering darkness. Addie remained on her steps, the business card cool between her fingers. Inside her bag, she could feel her sketchbook, that strange energy. No longer foreign, somehow part of her now.

Down the block, windows glowed with the comfortable routines of her neighbors—watching TV, reading bedtime stories settling in. Lives moving forward in familiar patterns while she prepared to step outside of time altogether.

All the places she could go. Coastal towns with dramatic skies. Bustling cities with their hidden pockets of need. Quiet villages where small changes might ripple outward for generations.

She could go anywhere, be anyone. The vastness of it was terrifying and intoxicating in equal measure.

The lilac crocuses at the edge of her lawn had closed their petals for the night. Tomorrow they would open again, for however long this false spring lasted. Always risky, blooming early.

Addie smiled.

She was ready to bloom.

So, so ready.

ALSO BY NICKY PENTTILA

Cosmic Weave

Cooperative Realm: Frankie's Journeys

Cargo Trouble

Frankie Takes a Holiday

Frankie Takes a Dive

Frankie Finds a Dot

Frankie Takes a Bow

Cargo & Chaos: Frankie books 1 & 2

Cooperative Realm: The Arkhide Chronicles

Hidden Planet

The Listeners

The Elders of Arkhide

Tales of Arkhide story collection

Short Stories

Here: Earthbound Fantasies and Futures

There: Journeys to Imagined Realms

Historical Fiction

A Note of Scandal

An Untitled Lady

The Spanish Patriot

ABOUT THE AUTHOR

Nicky Penttila wrote her first story, a Mayan murder mystery, in seventh grade. But then came gymnastics, math team, and boyfriends. Later came husband, car payments, and a sleep-depriving work schedule at newspapers across the country. Then came a second career as a science writer. But the fiction kept trickling out, a story here, a novella there, and finally, a real live novel. And she hasn't stopped.

Find more great reads at nickypenttila.com